To The Final End

Zora Stone

*For the ones who learned that choosing yourself isn't selfish.
It's survival. And for the eight idiots who refused to let go.*

PREVIOUSLY IN THE ETHER CHRONICLES

A quick refresher before we reach the final end

Welcome back, you gorgeous gluttons for emotional devastation! Ready to find out if love actually conquers all? Here's what you need to remember:

Shattering the Void: The Council brought five hundred soldiers to destroy everything Bree built. Ethos—wearing Phil's face like a cheap Halloween costume—came to finish what he started centuries ago.

The battle was chaos. Beautiful, terrifying chaos.

Seth wielded Void powers against the monster who'd trapped him. Riley's healed magic raced across the battlefield, buying precious seconds for the dying. Thane fell. Stellan fell. Everyone Bree loved was bleeding out on scorched earth.

So she did the only thing left to do.

She pushed *everything* out. Every drop of Ether. Every thread of silver light. Every piece of herself she'd been holding in reserve.

The blast shattered Ethos's hold on reality. The Void collapsed. The veins that threaded through the sanctuary—built from her own drained power—ignited in a column of white fire.

Her men breathed again.

She didn't.

Riley, dying ten feet away, used her last breath to save her sister: *"Touch her, you idiots."*

They formed a chain. Eight men. Eight bonds. Every hand on her skin, feeding power through Stellan as he tore the pain from her body and took it into himself.

Bree came back.

Riley didn't.

Welcome to **To the Final End.** Ethos is ash. The Void is gone. The sanctuary stands free for the first time in years.

But freedom isn't the same as healing. And some losses can't be undone.

The war is over. Now comes the harder part: learning how to live.

(Fair warning: bring tissues. Also wine. Possibly both at the same time.)

Content Warnings

This book contains themes and content that may be triggering to some readers. Please review the following warnings before proceeding:

Emotional & Psychological Themes

- **Death & Resurrection** – Protagonist experiences actual death and is brought back through magical intervention

- **Grief & Loss** – Death of a significant character; processing complicated feelings about someone who caused harm

- **Mass Casualties** – Seventeen funerals over one week; witnessing community-wide mourning

- **Survivor's Guilt** – Characters processing the cost of survival; questioning worthiness of being saved

- **Forgiveness of Abusers** – Complex exploration of forgiving someone who caused significant harm

- **Trauma Recovery** – Ongoing healing from captivity, magical violation, and near-death experiences

- **Time Skip Adjustment** – Four-year jump forward; adjusting to major life changes

Violence & Supernatural Threats

- **Battle Aftermath** – Dealing with destruction, casualties, and rebuilding after warfare

- **Character Death** – On-page death of a named character with emotional significance

- **Blood & Feeding** – Vampire-class feeding during intimate moments; consensual blood exchange

- **Near-Death & Resurrection** – Detailed depiction of dying and being pulled back through magical bonds

- **Physical Trauma** – Characters experiencing severe injuries; magical healing of broken bones

Intimacy & Relationships

- **Explicit Sexual Content** – Multiple detailed intimate scenes between consenting adults

- **Polyamorous Dynamics** – Romantic and sexual relationships with eight partners simultaneously

- **Group Intimacy** – Scenes involving multiple partners at once, including simultaneous penetration

- **Consensual Voyeurism** – Characters watching and being watched during intimate moments

- **Feeding During Intimacy** – Blood consumption during sexual encounters (consensual)

- **Magical Bonding** – Soul-deep connections formed and strengthened through physical intimacy

- **Male/Male Intimacy** – Romantic and sexual content between male characters

Dark Magic & Supernatural Elements

- **Magical Resurrection** – Being brought back from death through bond magic and life-force transfer

- **Pain Transfer** – Character absorbing another's suffering into themselves

- **Void Aftermath** – References to imprisonment in otherworldly dimension; lasting effects of Void corruption

- **Magical Purification** – Burning out corruption; intense physical transformation

Family & Community

- **Sibling Death** – Loss of a sister figure; complicated grief for someone who was both victim and perpetrator

- **Funeral Rituals** – Multiple on-page funeral scenes; preparing bodies for burial

- **Found Family** – Chosen family dynamics; building community from trauma survivors

- **Children in Epilogue** – Brief mentions of children in time-skip bonus content

- **Legacy of Abuse** – Processing the long-term impact of an abuser's actions on a community

Additional Notes

This book contains a hopeful ending and significant focus on healing, recovery, and building a life after trauma

The bonus epilogue (set four years later) contains extended explicit content with all partners

This list is provided to ensure a safe reading experience. If any of these topics are personally distressing, please read with care and compassion for yourself.

Thank you for completing this journey with Bree and her chosen family. You made it to the end.

Zora Stone

CONTENTS

Chapter 1
THANE

Dark.

Then not.

My eyes open to ash falling like snow.

For a moment I don't understand where I am. The sky is wrong—too bright, too silver, fractured with light that shouldn't exist. My chest doesn't move. My heart doesn't beat.

Then it does.

One brutal thud that cracks through my ribs like a fist.

I gasp. Choke. Claw at the dirt beneath me as my lungs remember how to work.

Dead.

The word surfaces before I can stop it.

I was dead. Not unconscious. Not fading. *Gone.*

I know the difference. I've walked the edge of it for centuries, fed from the dying, tasted the exact moment when life becomes absence. What I felt wasn't sleep.

It was nothing.

And then something dragged me back.

I force myself onto my elbows. The world tilts, stabilizes, tilts again. Blood in my mouth. Dirt under my nails. The thick, low hum of Ether gathering—too much of it, pressure building against my teeth like a coming storm.

Where is she?

My vision sharpens.

The courtyard is chaos. Bodies scattered across scorched ground. Some moving. Some not. The silver veins in the earth pulse like exposed arteries, brighter than I've ever seen them.

Then I find her.

Bree.

She's kneeling in the center of it all, hands buried in the dirt, head bowed. Silver mist pours from her like blood from an open wound—not curling, not drifting. *Flooding.* It streams into the veins beneath her, feeding something vast and hungry.

And ten feet in front of her—

Riley.

Kneeling the same way. Hands pressed to the ground. Black-silver Ether erupting from her palms, streaming toward Bree's light like a mirror reflection reaching for its source. Their magic meets in the space between them, twisting together, shadow and silver becoming something I don't have a name for.

Two halves of the same soul, facing each other across scorched earth.

My chest seizes.

I know what this is.

I've seen it once before. Centuries ago. A Source who gave too much. Who pushed everything she had into the world and burned herself hollow in the process.

She didn't survive.

"No—"

The word tears out of me. I shove to my feet. My legs don't want to hold me but I make them, staggering forward two steps before a hand catches my arm.

Stellan.

He's worse than I am—blood at his lip, one arm clutched against his ribs, face pale as bone. But his eyes are fixed on Bree with the same horror I feel clawing up my throat.

"She can't." His voice is harsh, cracking. "If she pushes everything—"

"I know."

"She'll be killed."

"I *know*."

I wrench free. Start moving. The ground pulses beneath my boots, Ether humming so loud I can feel it in my teeth. Every step closer to her, the pressure builds—not against me, but *through* me, like she's pulling from everywhere at once.

"Bree!"

She doesn't hear me. Doesn't look up. The silver in her mist is blinding now, too bright to look at directly.

I'm ten feet away when the veins ignite.

Light erupts from the ground in a column of white fire. The air splits. Sound dies. For one suspended heartbeat I see everything—Bree's face lifted toward the sky, Riley's hands locked in the dirt, their magic fused into something that screams through dimensions I can't name.

Riley's scream cuts through the light at the same moment mine does.

Then the blast hits.

White.

Everywhere.

I don't feel myself fly.

Sound returns first.

Screaming.

Not battle-screaming. Not pain. Something older. Something *wrong*.

Phil's voice—but not Phil's voice. The thing underneath, the presence that wore him like a mask, shrieking as if the light burned through layers of it.

Ethos.

Ethos is screaming.

I have never hated anything more than I hate him in this moment.

I force my eyes open.

The courtyard is scorched. Silver ash drifts through the air like the aftermath of a star dying. The veins in the ground have gone dark—not dead, but quiet. Waiting.

I'm on my back. Twenty feet from where I was standing.

Move.

I roll onto my side. Push up. My arms shake. My vision doubles, then corrects. The ringing in my ears drowns out everything except that horrible keening—Ethos still screaming, still too close to Bree, the sound getting weaker, fractured.

The wall where Seth stood is empty. Scorched stone. Nothing else.

Where is he?

I can't think about that now.

Bree.

I find her.

She's collapsed forward, face in the dirt. Hair covering her features. Hands still buried in the earth, but limp now—like the Ether burned straight through her and left the shell behind.

She's not moving.

Something inside me tears open.

"Bree—"

The word comes out broken. I don't recognize my own voice.

Not my queen. Not the Source. *Bree.*

Stellan appears beside me. On his knees. Breathing hard. His hand finds my shoulder—steadies me, barely. His eyes find her at the same time mine do.

I don't wait.

I don't think.

I shove to my feet and I move.

"We have to get to her."

It's not a command. It's not strategy. It's the only truth left in me—the only thing that matters in a world that just went white and silent and wrong.

Stellan doesn't argue. He's already moving too.

Ethos's screaming cuts off. But all I can focus on is her.

The silence that follows is worse.

Chapter 2
THEO

The world comes back in pieces.

Sound first—a ringing like glass shattering inside my skull. Then pressure. Weight across my chest, my ribs, my lungs struggling to expand.

I open my eyes.

White. Silver. Shapes that don't hold still.

My Seer vision strobes—silver threads cutting through shadow, flashes of possible futures burning into my retinas faster than I can process.

Then it clears.

Wes.

He's draped over me, arm flung across my chest, face pressed into the dirt beside my shoulder. Shielding me. Even unconscious, even blasted twenty feet from where we were—he put himself between me and the explosion.

"Wes." My voice comes out scraped raw. "Wes, wake up."

He groans. Shifts. His eyes open slowly, unfocused at first, then sharpening with something like panic.

"Bree—"

"I know." I push up, and he rolls off me, both of us struggling to our knees. "I know."

Movement to my left. Rhett coughs, rolls onto his side, fire sputtering weakly from his fingertips like a candle guttering in wind. He looks like hell—blood at his temple, ash in his hair, one arm hanging wrong.

But his voice is steady when he speaks.

"Get up." He forces himself to his feet. Sways. Stays upright. "Bree needs us."

I grab Wes's arm. He grabs mine. Rhett reaches down and hauls us both upright, and for a moment we're just three broken men holding each other together.

Then I see it.

The enemy army.

Five hundred soldiers who should still be charging. Who should be organizing, regrouping, pressing the advantage while we're scattered and broken.

They're not.

They're standing still.

Some look around wildly, weapons lowered, faces blank with confusion. Others are backing away—slow, uncertain steps like they've forgotten why they came. A cluster near the treeline has dropped to their knees, hands clutching their heads, mouths open in silent screams.

And the Feeders—the ones who marched with the Council, the ones bound by compulsion and threat—

They're blinking.

Hard. Rapid. Like waking from a nightmare they didn't know they were having.

"Why aren't they moving?" Rhett's voice is rough.

Wes stares at them. His hunger should be spiking—I can usually feel it radiating off him after a fight. But there's something steadier in him now. Something in his aura has shifted—purposeful, calm, as if whatever Bree did reached straight through the hunger and rewired it.

"It broke them," he whispers. "Her magic broke them."

Not killed.

Freed.

Even if only for a moment.

A voice cuts through the silence.

"Bree!"

Thane.

I've never heard him sound like that—raw, ragged, stripped of every layer of control he's spent centuries building. The name tears out of him like something breaking.

Rhett's head snaps toward the sound. His whole body goes rigid.

"Go." He shoves us forward. "Now."

We run.

Or something like running—stumbling, limping, dragging ourselves across scorched ground. Ahead, I can see Thane and Stellan already tearing toward the center of the blast, shadows against the silver ash.

My Sight tries to open again, but all I get is static—white, broken, useless.

The Council is scattered. Some fled—I catch glimpses of figures disappearing into the treeline. Others have fallen, motionless in the wreckage. A few stand frozen, staring at the place where Bree knelt like they've forgotten how to move.

The thing she was fighting—gone. Vanished.

Gray is dragging himself across the ground to my right—still in human form, one leg bent wrong, but moving. Pulling himself toward her with his hands, his elbows, whatever still works.

Zira stands over a Council enforcer, blood on her hands, eyes glowing. She doesn't look at us. Doesn't move. Just breathes.

Then I see Seth.

He's crumpled against the sanctuary wall, thirty feet from where Bree knelt. The Void energy that flickered around him is gone—no black threads, no silver lacing. But I think I see his chest move. Or maybe that's wishful thinking.

My chest seizes.

Is he—

I can't stop. Can't go to him. Bree first. Bree *first.*

We keep running.

The veins beneath our feet are dimming. I watch it happen—the silver light bleeding out of them step by step, fading from molten bright to dull gray. Like a heartbeat slowing. Like something vital draining away.

"The veins," Wes gasps. "They're going out."

"I see it."

We reach her.

Thane is already there, on his knees in the dirt. Stellan beside him. Stellan's hand trembles once—barely noticeable, gone in an instant—but I see it.

Neither of them is touching her. They're hovering—hands raised, frozen.

I skid to a stop. Drop to my knees across from them.

Bree is collapsed forward, face in the dirt. Hair covering her features. Hands still buried in the earth, but limp now. The silver mist that poured from her is gone.

She's not moving.

The air where she fell feels wrong—thin, hollow, like the world forgot how to breathe without her.

"Is she—" The question catches in my throat.

Thane's jaw works. His eyes are fixed on her, silver bleeding to gray. His hands shake. I've never seen Thane's hands shake.

"I don't know." The words come out broken, raw—nothing like the voice I've heard command armies and silence Council members. "I don't—"

He doesn't finish.

None of us touch her.

We just kneel there in the ash, in the silence, in the space where her magic used to be.

Waiting.

Hoping.

Terrified of what happens if we reach for her and find nothing.

Chapter 3
JACE

I wake up choking on ash.

My body jerks upright before my brain catches up—survival instinct, the one that's kept me alive through worse than this. Though honestly, I'm not sure I've *seen* worse than this.

The courtyard looks like the end of the world.

Silver ash drifting down like snow. Bodies scattered across scorched earth. The air tastes like ozone and blood and something else—something that burns at the back of my throat and won't go away.

I'm on my feet before I've finished processing any of it. Stopping means dying. Stopping means thinking. Neither of those is happening right now.

Bree.

She's at the center of everything. I can see the others already converging—Thane and Stellan closest, Theo and Wes and Rhett stumbling toward her from the opposite direction.

But Gray—

Gray is twenty feet to my left, dragging himself across the ground with his arms. One leg bent at an angle that makes my stomach turn. Human form, which means he either can't shift or won't, and neither option is good.

He snarls when I drop beside him. Actually *snarls*, lips pulling back from teeth that look too sharp for his current shape.

"Shut up." I loop his arm over my shoulders and haul him upright. He's heavy as hell and fighting me the whole way, because of course he is. "If you want to get to her alive, you need me."

The snarl dies. His weight settles against my side.

We move.

It's not fast. It's not pretty. But we make it—staggering across the blast radius until I can lower him next to the others. He collapses at Bree's side, one hand reaching toward her before he catches himself.

Nobody's touching her.

I file that away and turn back.

Seth.

He's crumpled against the sanctuary wall, thirty feet away. Too still. Too pale. The Void energy that was flickering around him during the fight is gone—no black threads, no silver lacing, nothing.

I run.

My knees hit dirt beside him. I press two fingers to his throat, searching—

There.

Faint. Thready. But there.

"You're not dying on me." I hook my arms under his and drag. His body is dead weight, heavier than it should be, but I've carried worse. "Not after all the shit we went through to find you."

Seth doesn't respond. Doesn't stir. But as I drag him across the battle-field, his body keeps trying to angle toward Bree—a slight pull, an unconscious lean, like something in him knows where she is even when he doesn't.

I don't have time to think about what that means.

I bring him to the circle and lower him gently on her left side. Gray is on her right. The others have gathered—Theo, Wes, Rhett, Thane, Stellan. All of them kneeling or crouching or hovering, none of them speaking.

None of them touching her.

The ground trembles.

I feel it through my knees—a shudder, a pulse, like the earth itself is gasping. The silver veins that thread through the stone beneath us flicker once.

Then they gutter.

Then they vanish.

Not fade. Not dim. *Vanish*—like ink sucked out of stone, like light pulled through a drain. One second they're there, pulsing with Bree's magic, and the next there's just... nothing.

Empty channels where power used to live.

"What the hell—"

I look up.

And I see him.

At the edge of the blast radius, where the worst of the damage hit. A silhouette—horned, silver-lined, shadow given shape.

Ethos.

Or what's left of him.

He's staring at Bree. At the place where the veins used to be. At the empty channels that fed into her hands.

His mouth opens.

"*What have you done?!*"

The words rip out of him—not smooth, not controlled, not the velvet manipulation I remember from the Void. This is raw. Furious. *Terrified.*

He doesn't get an answer.

He collapses inward.

It happens at the exact moment the last vein disappears—his form folding into itself like paper crumpling, like something vast being compressed into nothing. A final ripple of magic shudders through the air, pulls toward Bree, and then—

Gone.

I jerk in place. Look around.

No one else saw. They're all focused on her—on her stillness, her silence, the way she's not moving.

I open my mouth.

Close it.

I am not mentioning this. Not when everyone is barely standing.

Movement catches my eye. Stellan.

He's staring at Bree's hands—at the place where they're still buried in the dirt. His whole body has gone rigid, that careful control he wears like armor locked down so tight I can see the strain in his shoulders.

I follow his gaze.

Faint wisps of silver drift upward from the empty channels—barely visible, like smoke in moonlight. They pull toward Bree. Sink into her skin. Gather where her palms press into the earth.

I don't know what it means.

But Stellan does.

He goes very still. Not the controlled stillness I'm used to. Something else. Something that looks like horror wearing a mask of calm.

Why does he look like he just figured out something terrible?

I don't ask.

I kneel instead.

Gray on her right, one hand hovering near her shoulder. Seth on her left, unconscious but still angled toward her. Wes and Theo and Rhett gathered close. Thane shattered in a way I've never seen him. Stellan frozen, watching the silver wisps sink into Bree's skin.

And Bree.

Face down in the dirt. Hair covering her features. Hands limp in the earth.

Not moving.

The hollow pressure in the air makes it hard to breathe. The wrongness of her stillness makes it worse.

I place my hand on the ground near hers. Close, but not touching.

We all made it back to her.

Now she just has to come back to us.

A sound cuts through the silence. Weak. Wet. Wrong.

My head snaps up.

Riley.

She's ten feet away, collapsed where the blast threw her. Black-silver magic still flickers around her fingers, but it's guttering—dying. Her chest rises once. Barely. Then stutters.

She's fading.

But her eyes are open. Fixed on Bree. On the silver pooling into her sister's skin.

Her mouth moves.

"*Touch her.*" The words come out broken, barely a whisper. She drags in another breath—rattling, desperate. "*Touch her, you idiots.*"

Everyone freezes.

Riley's hand claws at the dirt, trying to drag herself closer. Failing.

"Her bonds—" Blood flecks her lips. "She needs to—*give* it somewhere—or it burns her—"

Her voice dies.

Her hand goes still.

Her eyes stay open, fixed on Bree.

And she doesn't breathe again.

Chapter 4
WES

There's a ringing in my ears that won't stop.

My body is shaking. I can't make it stop either.

Bree isn't moving.

Riley's eyes are still open. Still fixed on her sister. Still seeing nothing.

I look away. I can't—I can't watch her die twice.

The others are frozen around me. Gray trembling silently, one hand still hovering near Bree's shoulder. Jace staring straight ahead like if he blinks he'll shatter. Rhett's fire flickering at his fingertips—weak, useless, guttering out. Theo pale and wide-eyed, lips moving without sound. Thane's hands shaking so hard I can see it from here.

Stellan frozen. Watching something in the magic I can't see.

All of them.

Kneeling.

Waiting.

Doing *nothing*.

My chest caves in.

The hunger that's lived in me since I woke up wrong—since I started needing things I couldn't name—it collapses inward. Becomes something sharper. Something that feels like drowning.

Bree. No. No, no, no. Please no.

I can't lose her. I can't—

"What are we doing?"

The words come out broken. Barely audible.

No one hears me.

I try again. Louder. My voice shaking so hard the words almost don't form.

"What are we waiting for?"

Silence.

Something in me snaps.

"*What are we waiting for?!*"

My voice cracks. Raw. Unstable. I don't recognize the sound of it.

Everyone turns to look at me.

I jab a shaking finger at Bree.

"She's dying! She's—she needs—Riley told us—she said—"

I choke.

I can't finish.

Theo's voice comes quiet, steady. Repeating the words I couldn't get out.

"Touch her... or it burns her."

Stellan shifts. His voice is rough, stripped of its usual elegance.

"She's absorbing the Ether that kept the sanctuary alive. She'll rupture if she has nowhere to send it."

Jace's head snaps toward him. "But send it *where*—?"

Theo looks around at each of us. One by one.

"Us."

Gray makes a sound. Broken. Wounded.

Thane whispers, horrified. "It'll kill her if she tries to hold it alone."

My hands curl into fists. My whole body trembling.

"Then we don't let her do it alone."

The moment stretches.

No one moves.

The moment stretches.

No one moves.

Then Gray reaches first.

His hand trembles—I can see the effort it takes—but it lands on her shoulder. Solid. Committed.

Jace next. He presses his palm flat against her back, jaw tight.

Rhett sets two fingers over her wrist. His fire dies completely, but he doesn't pull away.

Theo cups the back of her hand. Gentle. Careful. Like she might break.

Thane touches the place over her spine. His eyes are closed. His lips move without sound.

Stellan's hand hovers. One breath. Two.

Then he commits.

Jace looks at Seth—still unconscious, still angled toward her like his body knows where she is even when his mind doesn't.

"He's bonded too." Jace's voice is rough. "He needs to be part of this."

He reaches over, takes Seth's limp hand, and places it against Bree's arm.

Seth's fingers twitch. Even unconscious, they curl toward her skin.

I wait until last.

My vision blurs. I don't bother wiping my face.

I place my palm over her heart.

Something clicks.

Soundless. Immense. Like reality itself acknowledging alignment.

The ground lights up.

Not the veins. Not the Ether pool.

Her.

Bree lights from inside—silver flooding her skin, spreading outward from where our hands touch. The glow pulses once, twice, then *surges.*

The magic hits us first.

I inhale sharply—all of us do—like being plunged into ice water. It rushes through my palm, down my arm, into my chest. Through the bond already formed.

The hunger that's lived in me since I woke—the ache, the emptiness, the constant *need*—

It fills with something unexpected.

With *her.*

Around me, the others gasp. React. Change.

Gray's leg snaps back into place with a crack that makes my stomach turn—but he doesn't scream. Just breathes. His whole body straightens.

Rhett's burns fade. The angry red skin smoothing over, healing in seconds.

Theo's eyes clear. The constant strain behind them—the pain of Sight that never stops—eases. He pulls his glasses off. No longer needed.

Jace's ribs knit. I hear them shift, settle, realign.

Thane's exhaustion vanishes. The gray pallor lifts from his skin. His silver eyes sharpen.

Stellan's magic stops fraying at the edges. I don't know how I know that, but I do—I can feel it, the way he stabilizes, calms.

Then Seth.

He arches off the ground.

Black smoke tears out of him—pouring from his mouth, his chest, the places where the Void corruption lived. Silver floods in behind it, filling the empty spaces, burning clean what was rotten.

His skin glows white-hot.

Then settles.

His first clear breath in months, maybe years escapes him with a gasp.

He slumps back—unconscious, but *clean*.

The magic pulls back.

Silence.

For one horrible moment, I think we failed.

Then—

Bree *inhales*.

Not soft. Not gentle.

A full, body-wracking, desperate breath—like someone who's been drowning finally breaking the surface.

Her fingers twitch.

Her chest rises again.

Something in my chest cracks open. My breath hitches—once, twice—and then my whole body is shaking, shoulders heaving, a sound tearing out of me that I don't recognize. The sob comes out silent but it wrecks me anyway, doubling me forward until my forehead nearly touches her shoulder. My hand stays pressed to her heart, feeling it beat—steady now, *real* now—while tears stream down my face and drip onto her shirt.

The others are reacting around me. Voices. Movement. Relief.

I don't hear any of it.

I lower my forehead to her shoulder.

"Don't ever do that to me again."

My voice cracks on every word.

Softer.

"*Please.*"

She doesn't answer.

But she breathes.

And thank the gods for that.

Chapter 5
STELLAN

She breathes.

The sound cuts through everything—the chaos, the voices, the ringing aftermath of magic that almost destroyed us all.

Bree *breathes*.

Every wall I've ever built collapses at once.

I thought I lost her. Thought *we* lost her. I was certain of it. Watching the silver pour into her skin, watching her collapse, watching the light leave—I was *certain*.

I'm moving before I've decided to move.

My hands find her shoulders. I pull her upright, pull her against my chest, wrap my arms around her like she might dissolve if I don't hold on hard enough. She's limp. Unconscious. But warm. *Alive.*

My hands are shaking.

I don't shake. I've spent centuries perfecting control, building walls so high and thick that nothing gets through. And now my hands are trembling against her back like I'm a child who's just watched the world end.

I bury my face in her hair.

She smells like ozone and ash and *her*—that impossible combination of vanilla and lightning that I've spent too long pretending doesn't affect me.

My magic flares.

Uncontrolled. Wild. Silver-white light pulses from my skin in erratic bursts, responding to the terror and relief and grief crashing through me in waves I can't stop.

That's when I feel it.

Nothing.

I'm touching her—holding her—and there's *nothing*.

No pull. No leash. No price.

The contract is gone.

Ethos is *gone*.

The realization hits like freedom. For centuries, every touch cost me. Every moment of connection, every feeding, every time I let myself want something—Ethos took his cut. The consequences were always there, waiting, a leash I couldn't see but always felt.

And now—

Nothing.

He's gone. The consequences died with him. Nothing can punish me for touching her now.

The grief surprises me. Ethos wasn't a monster to me—not only that, anyway. He was a constant. A master. The architecture my entire existence was built around.

And Bree destroyed him.

Saved me.

Almost died doing it.

I press my palm flat against her spine.

The pain hits me immediately.

Not a gentle siphon. Not the careful, regulated draw I've perfected. I rip myself open and *take*—brutal, unshielded, pulling everything she's carrying into myself with zero self-protection.

Her physical trauma floods in first. Bones that almost shattered. Muscles torn from channeling too much power. A body pushed past every limit it had.

Then the Ether strain. The impossible weight of absorbing magic that was never meant for one person to hold. The magic Ethos pulled from her for years while holding her captive.

Then the emotional overload. Fear. Grief. Determination. Love so fierce it burns.

I can feel Ethos's fingerprints on her soul, darkness she's been fighting since the first time he touched her mind.

It wrecks me.

My breathing stutters. My hands shake harder. My vision blurs at the edges, silver and black swimming together. I sink lower, my knees hitting the ground, but I don't let go.

I *can't* let go.

"Stellan—"

Someone's voice. Wes, maybe. I don't look up.

"He's taking it." Theo. Sharp. Alarmed. "He's draining her pain into himself."

"He's going to tear himself apart." Thane.

Hands reach for me. Someone grabs my shoulder.

I jerk away.

"*Don't.*"

The word comes out raw. Barely human.

I pull her closer. Tighter. My body curls around hers like instinct, like protection, like I can shield her from everything that's already happened if I just hold on long enough.

"Stellan." Thane's voice is closer now. Careful. "You can't take all of it. You'll—"

"I can take it."

"You'll kill yourself."

"*She can't hold this alone.*"

The pain burns through my veins. I can feel it tracing silver lines under my skin, visible now, glowing faintly in the dim aftermath of the blast. Every breath is agony. Every heartbeat pushes more of her suffering into my body.

I don't care.

I almost lost her. I will not lose her again.

"Let him." Wes's voice. Quiet. Understanding something the others don't. "But we feed him. So he can keep going."

I breathe deep.

Then I feel it—a hand on my shoulder. Solid. Warm. Magic flowing through the contact.

Thane.

He doesn't try to pull me away. Just anchors himself there, and I feel his power threading into me. Steadying. Strengthening.

Another hand—on Thane's shoulder. Rhett. Fire-warmth spreading through the chain.

Then Theo touching Rhett.

Jace touching Theo.

Wes touching Jace.

Gray last—one hand on Wes's shoulder, the other stretched toward Seth's unconscious form, completing some circuit I don't fully understand.

Magic flows.

Through the chain. Into me. Out of Bree as my magic pulls past breaking.

Silver and white light arcs between each touch point, visible threads connecting us all. I feel their strength pouring in—their power, their love for her, their desperate need for her to survive.

And still I take more.

I pull harder. The corruption burns as it passes through me—Void-dark and vicious, fighting every inch of the way. But I don't stop. I drag it out of her piece by piece, letting it shred me instead of her.

My body glows dangerously bright.

The pain is—

I can't describe the pain.

But her heartbeat strengthens under my palm.

Her breathing evens.

The frantic silver flickering under her skin begins to calm.

I take three more breaths of her agony.

Then I stop.

Not because I want to. Because there's nothing left to take.

She's stable.

She's *alive*.

My forehead drops to her hair.

I'm shaking so hard I can barely hold her. My magic flickers unsteadily, sparking and dying and sparking again. The chain behind me has gone quiet—hands still touching, but the desperate flow of power slowing to a trickle.

I should let go.

I should hand her to someone else—someone who hasn't just torn himself apart, someone who can actually take care of her.

I don't.

My arms tighten instead.

"Stay."

The word comes out broken. Barely a whisper against her hair.

"Please stay."

She doesn't answer.

But her heart beats steady against my chest.

And I am not letting go.

Chapter 6

BREE

I'm not dead.

That's the first thought. Stupid, maybe, but it's the one that surfaces as my lungs pull in air and my chest doesn't scream in protest.

I'm not dead, and I'm being held.

Arms around me. Warmth against my back. A heartbeat under my ear that isn't mine.

Stellan.

I know his scent before I open my eyes. Something expensive and sharp underneath the ash and blood and exhaustion.

My body feels... fine. Better than fine. The bone-deep drain I expected isn't there. I'm tired—gods, I'm tired—but it's the kind of tired that comes after a good cry, not after almost burning yourself alive channeling enough magic to level a city.

I healed them.

They healed me.

That's how this works now. I think I always knew that, somewhere underneath the fear. But knowing it and *feeling* it are different things.

I open my eyes.

They're all here.

Gray on my right, close enough to touch, one hand hovering near my shoulder like he's afraid I'll disappear if he blinks. His leg is straight again—healed—but his eyes are red-rimmed and raw.

Wes kneeling in front of me, face blotchy, tear tracks still wet on his cheeks. He's not trying to hide it. He's just looking at me like I'm the only thing in the world that matters.

Rhett beside him, hands still faintly warm, fire banked but steady. The burns on his arms are gone.

Jace a little further back, one hand on his knee, the other pressed flat against the ground like he needs to feel something solid. His ribs aren't broken anymore. I can tell by the way he's breathing.

Theo watching me with quiet awe, like he's seeing something no one else can.

Thane behind Stellan, silver eyes wet. *Wet.* I've never seen Thane cry.

And Seth—unconscious still, but breathing. The wrongness that clung to him is gone.

They're all looking at me.

I should say something. Something meaningful. Something that matches the weight of this moment.

Instead, I start crying.

Just... tears. Streaming down my face, dripping off my chin, and I can't stop them because I *saw*.

I saw everything.

I don't know how to explain it—I wasn't unconscious, not really. I was *there*, floating above myself, watching them fight for me. Watching Thane fall apart. Watching Wes scream. Watching Gray crawl. Watching Stellan wrap himself around my body like he could hold my soul in place through sheer force of will.

"I saw you."

The words come out rough. Broken.

Everyone goes still.

"I wasn't—" I swallow. Try again. "I wasn't gone. I was… above. Watching."

Wes makes a sound like I've just hit him.

"I saw what you did." I look at each of them in turn. "All of you. I felt it."

Gray's jaw tightens. Rhett looks away. Jace's hand curls into a fist against the ground.

But no one speaks.

"I knew you loved me." My voice cracks. I don't try to fix it. "I knew, even if you didn't say it. But I didn't—I didn't understand what that *meant*. Not until I watched you think I was gone."

Stellan's arms tighten around me. Barely. But I feel it.

"I'm here because of you." I reach out—toward Wes first, because he's closest, because his face is still wet, because he looks like he might shatter if I don't touch him soon.

My fingers brush his cheek.

He breaks. Folds forward, forehead dropping to my knee, shoulders shaking.

I let my hand rest on the back of his head. Look up at the others.

"I'm not going anywhere."

The words are simple. Quiet.

But I watch them land.

Gray shifts closer—finally touching me, hand on my shoulder, solid and warm. Rhett exhales shakily, his fire flaring once before settling. Jace wipes his face with the back of his hand and doesn't pretend he wasn't crying. Theo just nods, like he already knew.

Thane's shoulders drop. Something in his face loosens—not much, but enough.

And Stellan...

Stellan buries his face in my hair and breathes.

I let them hold me.

For the first time, I don't feel like a burden they're carrying.

I feel like the center of something. A circuit. A constellation. All of us connected, all of us holding each other up.

Then my eyes find Riley.

She's still. Ten feet away. Eyes open, fixed on nothing.

The tears change.

Not quiet anymore. Something deeper. Something that aches in a place I didn't know I had.

She saved me. Her last breath, her last words—*touch her, you idiots*—and she saved my life.

My sister.

The one I never got to know. The one who took my place and lived my life. The one who I chose to forgive. Though I'll never forget. The one who could have been my enemy and chose to be my salvation instead.

Gone.

Gray steps closer. Stellan's arms tighten. Wes lifts his head, sees where I'm looking, and his hand finds mine.

I don't have words.

I just cry.

And they let me.

Chapter 7
RHETT

She's awake.

She's crying. Talking. Reaching for the others.

She's *alive*.

The fire in my hands flickers back to life—not wild, not uncontrolled. Steady. Like it's syncing with her heartbeat.

I watch Stellan hold her. Watch her melt into him, exhausted and tear-streaked and so goddamn beautiful it hurts to look at her.

Even like this. Especially like this.

I almost lost her.

The thought keeps looping. Won't stop. My fire went out. My hands shook. I put two fingers on her wrist and felt *nothing* and I thought—

I can't think about what I thought.

I step forward.

Stellan sees me coming. His arms tighten around her for half a second—instinct, maybe, or reluctance—but when I rest my hand on his arm, something passes between us. Understanding. He releases her slowly.

I gather her into my chest.

She's warm. Breathing. *Here.*

My arms wrap around her so tight I'm probably hurting her, but I can't make myself loosen my grip. She doesn't fight it. Just sinks into me, her face pressed against my shoulder, her hands fisting in the back of my shirt.

"You scared the hell out of me."

The words come out rough. Barely above a whisper.

She laughs. Wet. Broken. "I know."

"Don't do that again."

"I'll try."

I press my forehead to hers. Close my eyes. Let myself have this one moment where she's safe and whole and mine.

Then I pass her to Gray.

He takes her like she's made of glass, but I see his shoulders shake when she wraps her arms around his neck. I turn away before I have to watch anyone else cry.

The battlefield is still.

I scan it properly for the first time since the blast. The courtyard is wrecked—scorched earth, silver ash, bodies scattered like broken toys. The veins that used to pulse through the ground are gone. Just empty channels where power used to live.

And the Feeders.

All of them. Ours and theirs. Standing in the wreckage like they've forgotten how to move.

The Council-bound ones look the worst—disoriented, blinking, some of them clutching their heads like they're fighting off a hangover. The compulsion that held them must have snapped when Ethos did.

Our Feeders are steadier, but not by much. They're watching Bree. Watching us. Glancing at Riley's body with expressions I can't read.

None of them know what comes next.

Neither do I.

Movement to my left. Seth.

He jerks awake with a gasp, eyes flying open, hands scrabbling at the dirt. For a second I tense—the last time he was conscious, Void energy was pouring out of him—but his eyes are clear. No black threads. No silver lacing.

Just panic.

"Where—" He tries to sit up. Falls back. "Bree?"

I kneel beside him. Offer my arm.

"She's okay." I keep my voice steady. "She's alive."

He grabs my forearm, grip weak but desperate. I haul him upright, keeping one hand on his shoulder to make sure he doesn't face-plant.

His gaze finds her immediately. Locked on like a compass finding north.

"She did it," he breathes. "She actually—"

"Yeah." I watch her move from Gray to Jace, accepting embrace after embrace. "She did."

I never thought I'd be helping him stand. But after today...

He's one of us now.

Bree finishes with Thane—his arms around her longer than anyone else's, his face buried in her hair—and finally steps back. She's steadier now. Still exhausted, still tear-streaked, but something in her spine has straightened.

She looks at me.

I tilt my head toward the watching Feeders.

"They're waiting for you."

Her gaze sweeps the courtyard. Takes in the scope of it—hundreds of faces turned toward her, silent and uncertain.

"All of them," I add. "They saw what happened. They need answers."

She nods slowly. Wipes her face with the back of her hand.

Then she sees Seth.

He's upright now, leaning on my arm, still pale and shaky but *awake*. Clear-eyed. Looking at her like she's the only thing in the world.

She runs.

Not walks. Not moves toward him carefully. She *runs*—tears still wet on her face, exhaustion forgotten—and slams into him hard enough that I have to brace them both.

Seth catches her. Barely. His arms wrap around her and he buries his face in her neck, and the sound he makes—raw, broken, relieved—is the same one I was choking back five minutes ago.

"You're okay," she whispers. "You're *you* again."

"Because of you." His voice cracks. "Bree—"

"I know." She pulls back just enough to cup his face, thumbs brushing his cheekbones. "I know."

The Feeders are watching. Hundreds of them. Waiting for their queen to address them, to tell them what happens next.

And she's standing in the wreckage of a battlefield, holding a man with magic from the Void, crying into his shirt like nothing else matters.

Because to her, it doesn't.

We come first.

The politics can wait.

She kisses Seth's forehead. Whispers something I can't hear. Then she steps back, squeezes his hand once, and finally turns toward the crowd.

Now she's ready.

She walks forward.

We fall into formation without discussing it. Gray on her right. Me on her left. Stellan at her shoulder. Thane opposite. Wes and Jace flanking Seth, helping him stay upright. Theo between groups, watching everything with those Seer eyes.

The Feeders part as we approach. They don't kneel, but they don't run either. They just... wait.

Bree stops at the center of the courtyard. Looks around at the faces watching her.

And she tells them the truth.

"You were deceived."

Her voice carries. Stronger than I expected. The crying girl from five minutes ago is gone—this is something else. Something harder.

"All of you. For the past year."

She pauses. Her gaze moves to Riley's body. Still. Silent. Eyes fixed on nothing.

"The woman who ruled here while I was gone—the one who wore my face and gave orders in my name—was not me."

The silence shifts. Sharpens.

"Her name was Riley. She was my mirror-self. My sister." Bree's voice wavers, but she doesn't stop. "She was manipulated. Used. Ethos pulled her out of the Void and put her in my place while I was trapped. Everything she did here—the cruelty, the control, the things done in my name—that was his design. Not hers."

She takes a breath "And not mine."

She looks back at the crowd.

"She died saving my life. Her last breath was spent telling these men, my men, how to keep me alive." Bree's jaw tightens. "Whatever you think of her, whatever she did while wearing my face—she was a victim too. And in the end, she chose me over him."

Some of the Feeders glance at Riley's body. Others stare at Bree like they're seeing her for the first time.

"Phil was never Phil." Bree continues. "He was Ethos. The thing that's been pulling strings from the Void for centuries. The Council's puppet master. The reason Feeders have been hunted and enslaved and treated like weapons instead of people."

She turns to Stellan.

He steps forward. His voice is quiet, but it cuts through everything.

"Ethos is dead. I can confirm it—I watched him collapse. The contract that bound him to this me is gone." He pauses. "I felt it break."

Bree looks at Seth.

He moves to her side, still unsteady, still pale. But his voice is clear.

"The Void is no more. Ethos's realm collapsed when Bree overloaded the network." He swallows. "She didn't just kill him. She destroyed everything he built. There's nothing left."

Silence. Complete.

Bree lets it stretch. Then she speaks again.

The Feeders stare. Some of them look terrified. Some look awed.

"You have a choice."

Her voice is softer now. But no less certain.

"You *always* have a choice. Take the Oath or don't. Stay or don't. Follow me or find your own way." She pauses. "You are free."

Something shifts in the crowd. I see it happen—shoulders dropping, breath releasing, the tension of years of compulsion finally letting go.

"I will rebuild," Bree continues. "I will make things right. For every Feeder who was abandoned. For every life Ethos touched. For all of you."

She's not asking for loyalty. She's not demanding anything.

She's offering.

And from the looks on their faces, they're going to take it.

Movement.

My head snaps toward the treeline. Someone slipping away—a figure in Council robes, moving fast and quiet through the shadows.

"Bree."

She follows my gaze. Sees.

But Zira is faster.

She materializes out of nowhere—blood still on her hands, eyes still glowing—and steps directly into the runner's path.

"Going somewhere?"

The figure freezes.

I recognize her now. Eris. The Seer-councilor. Eyes blank and silver, face carefully neutral.

Bree walks toward her. Steady. Unhurried.

The rest of us follow.

Eris doesn't run. She can't—Zira's blocking the only exit, and we're closing in from the other side.

Bree stops three feet away.

"Hello, Eris."

The councilor's expression doesn't change. "Source."

"You knew." It's not a question.

Eris tilts her head. "I see many things. Not all of them are clear until they happen."

"You saw this?"

A pause. "I saw... possibilities."

"And you did nothing."

Another pause. Longer this time.

"I did what I could."

Bree stares at her. The silence stretches.

Then she steps aside.

Eris blinks. For the first time, something like confusion flickers across her face.

"Go."

"You're... releasing me?"

"I'm letting you run back to whatever's left of your Council." Bree's voice is steady. Cold. "Though it might just be you."

She takes a step closer. Eris flinches.

"I'm not sure we need a Council anymore. Not the way it was. Not with the people who let this happen." Bree tilts her head. "It's time to rebuild something better."

Eris stares at her.

"Go," Bree repeats. "Before I change my mind."

The Seer doesn't need to be told twice. She slips past Zira—who looks deeply disappointed—and disappears into the treeline.

Zira watches her go, then turns to Bree. "You sure about that?"

Bree's mouth curves. Not quite a smile.

"She doesn't have anything left."

Chapter 8
BREE

I've been showered for an hour.

Clean clothes. Pajamas that someone left outside my door—soft cotton shorts and a worn tank top that smells like lavender. My hair is still damp, leaving wet patches on my shoulders.

I should be sleeping. Everyone else is. The sanctuary has gone quiet in that heavy, exhausted way that comes after something terrible. The guys are scattered in their rooms nearby—I can feel them through the bonds, dim pulses of warmth that tell me they're alive, resting, healing.

But I can't close my eyes without seeing Riley's face.

So I'm wandering.

The hallway outside is empty. Moonlight spills through the windows, casting pale squares on the stone floor. My bare feet make no sound as I walk.

That's when I see him.

Seth.

He's stepping out of the bathroom at the end of the hall, towel wrapped low around his hips, water still dripping from his hair onto his shoulders. He looks... different. Cleaner than just the shower. Like the Void residue that clung to him has finally been scrubbed away—inside and out.

He stops when he sees me.

For a moment, we just stand there. Twenty feet apart. Him half-naked and dripping, me in pajamas with wet hair.

My eyes trace the water sliding down his chest before I can stop them.

"Hey," I say.

"Hey." His voice is rough. He clears his throat. "I was just—" He gestures vaguely toward a door. His room, I guess.

"I know." I take a step closer. "Can we talk?"

Something shifts in his expression. Careful. Guarded. Like he's bracing for bad news.

"Yeah. Of course."

He pushes open the door and holds it for me. I slip past him into the room—small, simple, a bed with fresh sheets and a window letting in moonlight. Someone's left clean clothes folded on a chair.

Seth grabs them, hesitates.

"I should probably—"

"It's fine." I sit on the edge of the bed, pulling my knees up. "I've seen worse."

He huffs out something that's almost a laugh. Turns his back to me and drops the towel.

I watch.

I can't help it. The moonlight catches the planes of his back, the dip of his spine, the curve of muscle as he steps into clean pants and pulls them up over his hips. He doesn't bother with a shirt.

When he turns around, he catches me looking.

Neither of us pretends I wasn't.

He leans against the wall across from the bed, arms crossed over his bare chest. Waiting.

The silence stretches.

"You were out for most of it," I finally say. "After the blast."

He nods slowly. "I remember pieces. The light. You on the ground. And then—" He frowns. "Hands. Everyone touching you. Magic flowing."

"The healing chain. The guys fed Stellan power so he could pull the pain out of me."

"And me?"

"Jace put your hand on my arm. Even unconscious, you reached for me." I swallow. "You were part of it, Seth. Part of what brought me back."

His jaw tightens. He looks away.

"I woke up and you came to me." His voice is quiet. "In the courtyard. Before you talked to the Feeders. You ran to me."

"I did."

"Why?"

The question hangs between us.

"Because I needed to." I pull my knees closer to my chest. "Because when I saw you awake—really awake, and alive—something in me just... broke. I had to touch you. Had to make sure you were real."

He's quiet for a long moment.

"I thought I died." The words come out rough. Scraped raw. "In the blast. When the light hit. I thought that was it. And I was—" He stops. Starts again. "I was okay with it. Because at least you'd be free. At least Ethos would be gone."

"Seth—"

"I didn't think I deserved to come back." He finally looks at me. His eyes are wet. "After everything. The Void. What it did to me. The things I went through. I thought—"

"Stop."

I stand. Cross the room. He tenses as I get closer, but he doesn't move away.

I stop right in front of him. Close enough to feel his warmth radiating off his bare skin.

"You didn't deserve any of that," I tell him. "Ethos was a monster. And he's gone now. You felt it collapse, didn't you? The Void?"

He nods. Barely.

"Then you know. It's over. He's gone. And you're *here*." I reach up and touch his face. His jaw. The curve of his cheekbone. His skin is warm and still slightly damp from the shower. "You came back to me."

His breath catches.

"The bond," he whispers. "I felt it. In the Void. When you claimed me. I didn't understand what it was—I just knew I had to get to you. That something was pulling me toward you and I couldn't stop it."

"Did you want to stop it?"

He shakes his head slowly. "No."

"Good." My thumb brushes his lower lip. I feel him shudder. "Because I chose you, Seth. In the Void, when I didn't even know what I was doing. My Ether chose you before my mind caught up."

"Bree—" His voice breaks. "You don't have to—I know you have the others. I'm not expecting—"

"I already chose you."

The words hang between us.

His whole body goes still.

"I ran to you first," I continue. "Before I faced the Feeders, before I dealt with any of it. I saw you and I ran. Because you come first. All of you. But especially—" I take a breath. "You were in the Void with me. You found me when I was lost. You stayed when you could have run."

"I couldn't leave you." His voice is raw. "Even when I had to, it was only to find a way to get you out."

"I know."

I step closer. Press my body against his bare chest. Feel his heart hammering through both our skins.

His hands come up—tentative, shaking—and settle on my waist. His fingers flex against the thin cotton of my tank top.

"Is this—" He swallows. "Are you sure?"

"Yes."

"I haven't—" He stops. Tries again. "Not since before. Not since before the Void. I don't know if I can—"

"Then we figure it out together."

I rise up on my toes and kiss him.

His mouth opens under mine immediately.

Not hesitant. Not careful. *Hungry.*

His hands tighten on my waist, pulling me flush against him. I feel every inch of his bare chest through my thin tank top—the heat of him, the hard planes of muscle, the way his heart pounds against mine.

I slide my hands up his chest, feeling him shiver under my palms. Over his shoulders. Into his still-damp hair.

He groans into my mouth.

The sound goes straight through me. My fingers tighten in his hair and I pull, tilting his head back so I can deepen the kiss. His hips buck forward involuntarily and I feel him—hard already, straining against the thin fabric of his pants, pressing into my stomach.

"Bree—" He breaks the kiss, breathing ragged. "I need—I want—"

"Tell me."

His eyes are dark. Desperate. "You. Just you."

I pull back just enough to grab the hem of my tank top. His gaze drops to my hands, tracking the movement.

I pull it over my head.

His breath punches out of him.

I'm not wearing anything underneath. The cool air hits my bare skin and my nipples tighten. Seth stares at me like I've just handed him something sacred.

"God." The word comes out reverent. Broken. "Bree, you're—"

"Touch me."

His hands shake as he lifts them. They hover over my breasts for a moment—hesitating, uncertain—until I grab his wrists and place his palms flat against my chest.

We both inhale sharply.

His hands are warm. Rough. They span almost the entire width of my ribcage, fingers curling around my sides while his thumbs brush the undersides of my breasts.

"Is this—"

"More."

He cups me properly then, thumbs dragging over my nipples. I arch into the touch, gasping, and he does it again—watching my face, learning what makes me react.

"Like that?" he whispers.

"*Yes.*"

He lowers his head.

The first touch of his mouth on my breast makes my knees buckle. He catches me—one arm wrapping around my waist to hold me up while his lips close around my nipple and *suck.*

"*Seth—*"

He groans against my skin. The vibration shoots straight to my core. His tongue circles and flicks while his other hand palms my neglected breast, pinching and rolling until I'm writhing against him.

I need more. I need—

I reach between us and palm him through his pants.

He jerks like I've shocked him. Hips bucking forward, pushing himself harder into my hand. A broken sound tears out of his throat.

"Bed," I manage. "Now."

He walks me backward without breaking contact. My calves hit the mattress and I fall back, pulling him down with me. He catches himself on his forearms, hovering over me, and for a moment we just breathe.

His eyes trace my face. My bare chest. The way I'm spread beneath him.

"You're sure?" he asks again.

I reach down and push at his pants. "Get these off."

He scrambles to obey. Kicks the pants off somewhere onto the floor. When he settles back over me, there's nothing between us but my shorts.

I feel him against my thigh. Hard and hot and *big*—bigger than I expected—and my whole body clenches with want.

His hips roll once. Involuntary. The friction drags a moan out of both of us.

"I want to taste you," he breathes. "Can I—please—"

"*Yes.*"

He slides down my body. Hooks his fingers in my shorts and pulls them down my legs, taking my underwear with them. I'm completely bare beneath him now, and he stares at me like he's memorizing every inch.

"Beautiful," he whispers. "You're so fucking beautiful."

Then he lowers his head between my thighs.

The first stroke of his tongue makes me cry out. My hands fly to his hair, gripping hard, and he groans against me—the vibration sending shockwaves through my entire body.

He licks me like he's starving. Long, slow strokes that drag through my wetness and circle my clit before pulling away. Again and again until I'm shaking, until my thighs are trembling on either side of his head, until I'm making sounds I don't recognize.

"Seth—I need—*please*—"

He slides two fingers inside me.

I shatter.

The orgasm rips through me without warning—my back arching off the bed, my hands fisting in his hair, his name tearing out of my throat. He works me through it, tongue still moving, fingers curling against that spot inside me that makes stars burst behind my eyes.

When I finally come down, he's pressing soft kisses to my inner thighs. Waiting.

"Get up here," I manage.

He crawls up my body. His cock drags against my leg, my hip, my stomach—leaving a wet trail that makes me clench with anticipation. When his face is above mine, I pull him down and kiss him, tasting myself on his tongue.

"I need you inside me," I whisper against his mouth. "Now."

He reaches between us. I feel the head of him notch against my entrance and we both freeze.

"Bree—" His voice is wrecked. Shaking. "I don't know if I can control the feeding. Not with you. Not when it matters this much."

I cup his face in my hands. Make him look at me.

"Then don't control it. Let it happen. I trust you."

His eyes close. A full-body shudder runs through him.

Then he pushes inside.

The stretch is almost too much.

He's bigger than I'm used to—my body resists for a moment before something releases and he slides deeper. I gasp. He freezes.

"Okay?" His voice is tight. Controlled. "Am I hurting you?"

"No. Don't stop. *Don't stop.*"

He presses forward. Inch by inch. Filling me so completely I can't breathe. When he's finally seated all the way inside me, we both go still.

His forehead drops to mine. His whole body is trembling.

"*Fuck,*" he breathes. "You feel—I can't—"

"Move."

He pulls back slowly. Pushes in again. The drag of him inside me sends sparks shooting up my spine.

"More," I demand. "*Harder.*"

He obeys.

His hips snap forward and I cry out—pleasure and fullness and the perfect edge of too much. He sets a rhythm that has me clawing at his back, wrapping my legs around his waist, pulling him deeper with every thrust.

The bond flares between us.

I feel it like a physical thing—silver light pulsing in my chest, reaching for him, wrapping around us both. And underneath it, something else. His hunger. Something older. Darker. The vampire in him waking up.

His mouth drags down my throat. Open. Hot. His breath comes in harsh pants against my pulse point.

"Bree—" His voice is wrecked. Desperate. "I need—I can feel it—I don't want to hurt you—"

"You won't."

He shifts angles and hits something inside me that makes my vision white out. I dig my nails into his shoulders and he hisses, hips stuttering, mouth still pressed to my neck.

"Right there," I manage. "*There.*"

He drives into that spot over and over. The pleasure builds—a wave cresting higher and higher—and I can feel him getting close too, his rhythm faltering, his fangs scraping my skin without breaking it.

"I can't—" He's shaking. Fighting himself. "Bree, I'm going to—I need to—"

"Then take it."

I turn my head. Bare my throat completely.

"*Take what you need.*"

He shatters.

His fangs sink into my neck at the same moment his hips slam home one final time. The pain is bright, sharp, immediate—and then it transforms. Pleasure floods through me, liquid and hot, tangling with the orgasm that crashes through my body without warning.

I scream his name.

He drinks.

I feel everything—his hunger finally being fed, his relief, his overwhelming *gratitude*. The bond blazes between us, my Ether rises to meet his pull, feeding him willingly, and I wouldn't have it any other way.

He pulses inside me. I clench around him. The feeding amplifies every sensation until I can't tell where the orgasm ends and the blood-bond begins.

His pulls are deep. Greedy. Starving.

Then they slow.

Gentle. Savoring. He licks across the wound, sealing it, and I feel the sting fade to warmth. His hips are still pressed flush against mine, both of us trembling with aftershocks.

He pulls back just enough to look at me.

Blood stains his lips. His eyes are wild—blown dark with pleasure and something like awe.

"Did I—" He swallows hard. "Are you—"

I pull him down and kiss him.

I taste copper. Salt. *Us.*

"I'm perfect," I whisper against his mouth. "You're perfect."

A sound tears out of him. Something broken almost like he's becoming something new.

We collapse together.

After, he buries his face in my neck.

His whole body is shaking. Not from exertion. Something deeper.

"Thank you," he whispers.

I run my fingers through his hair, still damp with sweat now instead of shower water. "For what?"

"For choosing me." His voice cracks. "I didn't think—I didn't think anyone would ever want me again. Not after being trapped for so long. Losing what I was."

My chest aches.

I pull him closer. Feel him still softening inside me, neither of us ready to separate yet.

"You're mine, Seth." The words come out steady. Certain. "You always were. Even before you knew it."

He makes a sound against my skin.

I press a kiss to his temple. Feel the bond humming between us—settled now, content, complete.

"We come first," I tell him. "All of us. That's how this works."

He lifts his head. Looks at me with wet eyes and a trembling smile.

"Yeah." He breathes. "I'm starting to get that."

He pulls out gently—we both wince at the loss—and settles beside me, pulling me into his chest. I press my cheek against his heartbeat.

Outside, the sanctuary is figuring out how to exist in a world without Ethos.

But here, in this small room, with this man who came back from the Void for me—

Everything is exactly right.

Chapter 9

BREE

Something's pressing on my bladder.

That's the first thing I register. Not the warmth, not the safety, not the seven heartbeats surrounding me—just the urgent need to pee and the complete impossibility of moving.

I crack one eye open.

Wes is the bladder problem. He's sprawled across my stomach like he's trying to become part of me, cheek mashed against my ribs, drooling slightly.

Lovely.

Gray has my legs pinned. Both of them. He's curled around my calves like I might try to escape in the night, and honestly, with his grip, I couldn't if I wanted to.

Jace is snoring into my hair. I can feel each exhale, hot and damp against my scalp. His arm is flung across the pillow above my head, and at some point in the night, I apparently became his teddy bear.

Rhett's hand is on my hip. Heavy. Warm. Even in sleep, he runs hot—I can feel the heat radiating off him through my clothes.

Theo's fingers rest against my pulse point. Light enough that I almost don't notice. He does this sometimes. Checks that I'm still here.

Seth's face is pressed to my shoulder, his breath slow and even. The bite mark on my neck throbs faintly when I shift—healed but not forgotten. His hand rests over my heart like he fell asleep counting the beats.

Thane is on his back at the edge of the bed. Still as death. But I feel him through the bond—awake, watching, waiting for me to open my eyes.

And Stellan—

Stellan is sitting at the foot of the bed, back against the frame, watching me with that unreadable expression he does so well.

"Morning," I croak.

"You've been awake for three minutes." His voice is soft. "I was timing how long you'd pretend to sleep."

"I wasn't pretending. I was accepting my fate."

His mouth twitches.

The bed is huge. Stupidly huge. It wasn't this big a week ago—I remember because I used to be able to touch both edges if I stretched. Now there's room for nine bodies with space to spare.

The sanctuary did this. Reshaped itself around us while we slept, grew the bed, expanded the walls. Like it knew what I needed before I did.

I should probably be used to it. I'm not.

A week.

It's been a week since the blast. Since Ethos. Since Riley bled out ten feet in front of me while I lay helpless on the ground.

A week of cleaning debris from hallways and scrubbing blood from stone. A week of Feeders showing up confused and starving, their compulsions shattered, wandering around like they'd just woken from a nightmare. Which, I guess, they had.

A week of funerals.

Seventeen of them.

Seventeen Feeders who didn't survive the blast, the battle, the chaos. Some died fighting for Ethos's army. Some died fighting against it. Some just got caught in the crossfire—wrong place, wrong time, wrong everything.

We went to every single one.

Me and the guys, showing up at dawn burials and sunset pyres, standing with families who didn't expect us, holding space for grief that wasn't ours but somehow became ours anyway. I didn't give speeches. Didn't try to explain or justify or make it better. I just showed up.

Thane said it mattered. That seeing me there, seeing all of us there, changed something in the way the sanctuary Feeders looked at me.

I don't know if that's true. I just know that those seventeen people deserved to be mourned. Deserved witnesses. Deserved someone to remember their names.

Today is eighteen.

Today is Riley.

The thought slides into my chest like cold water.

Wes shifts against my stomach, mumbling something. Gray's grip tightens on my legs. Jace's snoring hitches. They feel it too. The bond carries everything—my grief bleeding into theirs, pulling them toward consciousness whether they want it or not.

Rhett's hand flexes on my hip. His eyes open.

"Hey." His voice is rough with sleep.

"Hey." He searches my face. Finds what he's looking for.

"Today?" he asks.

I nod.

That's all it takes.

One by one, they wake. Gray lifts his head from my legs, blinking. Wes groans and rolls off my stomach, freeing my bladder—finally. Jace stops snoring mid-breath and mutters something obscene. Theo's fingers tighten on my wrist before letting go.

Seth presses a kiss to my shoulder. Doesn't say anything. He doesn't need to. Thane watches me sit up slowly, silver eyes finding mine across the room.

"We're ready when you are," he says.

I look at all of them. My men. My family. The people who've stood beside me through seventeen funerals this week, who held my hand while I watched strangers burn, who never once complained about the early mornings or the long silences or the way I sometimes cried in the shower afterward.

"I need to pee first," I say. Jace snorts.

"Way to ruin the moment."

"The moment can wait. My bladder can't."

I extract myself from the bed—it takes longer than it should, everyone reluctant to let go—and pad to the bathroom on bare feet.

When I close the door behind me, I let myself breathe.

Just for a second.

Then I splash water on my face and go back out to face the day.

The sanctuary grounds don't look like a graveyard anymore.

A week ago, this courtyard was a battlefield. Bodies everywhere. Blood soaking into the stone. The silver veins pulsing with stolen Ether, spreading like infection through every crack.

Now—

Gardens. They're back, finally. The magic that created them when I first came to the Sanctuary the first time are in full bloom again. Feeders working side by side, hauling debris, repairing walls, stringing lights between the rebuilt columns. Children running between the adults, shrieking with laughter, completely unaware that a week ago this place was hell.

The veins are gone. Just... gone. When I pushed my power through, and then pulled all that Ether back into myself, they disappeared and didn't come back. The stone where they used to pulse is smooth now. Clean.

New.

I've watched it transform all week. Between funerals, between rebuilding, between falling into bed exhausted and waking up surrounded by warmth. Every day the sanctuary looks a little more alive, a little more like what it was supposed to be. The Ether working in tandem with everyone.

Pride swells in my chest. And underneath it, an ache so sharp I have to press my hand to my sternum.

Riley won't see this.

She spent five years ruling this place with fear and black Ether and my stolen face. Five years watching it crumble while she pretended to rebuild. Five years destroying the people who trusted her because Ethos had his hooks so deep she couldn't tell where he ended and she began.

And now it's finally becoming something real—and she's not here to see it.

I don't know if she would have wanted to. I don't know if she would have cared.

But I think, somewhere underneath all that armor, there was a version of Riley who wanted this. Who wanted peace instead of power, connection instead of control.

Ethos never let her find out.

"I want to do it myself."

The guys exchange looks. The kind that says is she serious and should we stop her and she's definitely serious, don't even try.

"Bree." Theo's voice is gentle. "You don't have to—"

"I know I don't have to." I look at the closed door in front of me. The room where they've been keeping her body, preserved by Ether, waiting. "I want to."

We've done this seventeen times this week. Stood in cold rooms with cold bodies, helped families prepare their dead for burning. Theo knows the prayers now. Rhett can light a pyre without flinching. Jace has stopped making inappropriate jokes—mostly.

But this one is different.

This one is mine.

More looks.

Thane steps forward. "We'll be right outside."

I nod.

He opens the door for me. I walk through.

She looks like me.

That's the first thing I think, standing over her body. She looks like me, but wrong. Like a photograph that's been slightly overexposed. The same features, the same hair, the same shape of her face—but something essential missing.

She's on a stone table. Clean white cloth beneath her. Someone washed the blood off, closed her eyes. But no one touched her beyond that.

They were waiting for me.

I move closer.

Her skin is cold when I touch her face. Of course it is. She's been dead for a week. But it still shocks me—the absence of warmth, of life, of the fire that burned in her even when that fire was pointed at me.

"Hey," I whisper.

Stupid. Talking to a corpse. She can't hear me.

I do it anyway.

"I'm sorry."

My hands shake as I dip a cloth in the basin someone left on the table. Warm water. Herbs floating in it—lavender, rosemary. Things that smell like peace.

I wash her face. Slowly. Carefully. The same way someone should have washed mine, all those years ago, when I was the one broken and bleeding.

"I'm sorry I didn't save you sooner. I'm sorry I didn't see what he was doing to you. I'm sorry you spent five years wearing my face and hating every second of it."

The water turns pink. There's still blood in her hair, dried and crusted at her temples. I work it out strand by strand.

"You weren't evil." My voice cracks. "I know everyone thinks you were. I know you thought you were. But you weren't. You were just another girl he stole. Another girl he broke."

I've said versions of this seventeen times this week. Standing over bodies I didn't know, speaking to families who blamed themselves, trying to find words for grief that doesn't make sense.

This is the first time I've said it and meant it for myself.

I braid her hair the way I braid mine—simple, practical, out of her face. She never wore it like this. She always left it loose, flowing, dramatic. But this feels right.

This feels like giving her back something he took.

"You saved me." I tie off the braid with a strip of cloth. "At the end. When it mattered. You told them how to bring me back." My throat tightens. "You didn't have to do that. You could have let me die and taken everything. But you didn't."

I dress her in clean clothes. Simple ones—a soft dress in pale gray, nothing fancy. She would have hated it. She liked bold colors, statement pieces, things that demanded attention.

But I think, underneath all that armor, she wanted to rest.

So I give her rest.

"I forgive you," I whisper.

The words hang in the cold air.

I don't know if they're true. I don't know if forgiveness works that way—if you can just decide and have it be real. Maybe I'll wake up tomorrow and hate her again. Maybe I'll spend years working through what she did to my life, to my men, to me.

But right now, standing over her body with wet hands and a cracked-open chest—

I mean it.

The courtyard is full. I stop dead in the doorway, Riley's body in my arms, and stare.

I expected the guys. Maybe Zira. Maybe a handful of the Feeders who'd been at the other funerals this week, the ones who seemed to understand what I was trying to do.

Not this.

Hundreds of them.

Every Feeder in the sanctuary, from the looks of it. Standing in neat rows across the courtyard, heads bowed, silent. Waiting.

My breath catches.

These are the Feeders who lived under Riley's rule for five years.

The ones she enslaved. Manipulated. Controlled with black Ether and whispered lies. The ones who thought they were serving me while she used my face to break them. The ones who flinched when she walked by, who couldn't look her in the eye, who woke up screaming because they couldn't tell the difference between me and her.

They have every reason to hate her.

Every reason to spit on her grave, to curse her name, to celebrate her death.

And they're here.

"Bree." Seth's hand on my back. Steady. "They wanted to come."

"I didn't—I didn't ask them to—"

"You didn't have to." I look at him. At all of them—my men flanking me like an honor guard, faces solemn.

"They've been watching you all week," Thane says quietly. "Every funeral. Every family. You showed up for strangers, Bree. For people you'd never met, people who died fighting on both sides." His jaw tightens. "They noticed."

"And you asked them to forgive," Stellan adds, his voice low. "Not demanded. Asked. Explained Riley acted because Ethos got to her." He pauses. "Some of them aren't ready. Some of them may never be. But they came anyway."

I scan the crowd.

Some faces are wet with tears—and I don't think they're tears of grief. Some are hard, closed off, jaws tight with the effort of being here. A few won't meet my eyes at all. I see hands clenched into fists, shoulders rigid with tension, mouths pressed into thin lines.

They're not here because they forgave her.

They're here because they're trying.

Because I asked.

Because showing up to seventeen funerals for their people meant something.

Because grace is a choice you make over and over, especially when it hurts.

"For you," Stellan says. "They came for you."

My eyes burn.

This is what I wanted. What I asked for. What I begged them to consider in the hours after the battle, when anger was still hot and vengeance felt justified.

She was a victim too. He broke her the same way he tried to break all of us. The only difference is he got to her first.

I didn't know if they believed me. I didn't know if it mattered.

Apparently, it did.

My hands shake as I carry her forward.

The pyre is beautiful.

Wooden beams stacked high in the center of the courtyard. Flowers woven through the structure—white lilies, purple heather, something golden I don't recognize. The Feeders must have gathered them.

Not because they loved Riley.

Because they love me.

Or because they're trying to. Because they want to believe in something better than what they had. Because showing up is the first step toward healing, even when you're not sure you want to heal.

I lay Riley on top gently. Arrange her hands over her chest. Smooth a strand of hair back from her face.

Then I step back.

Gray moves first.

He places a carved stone at her head—a wolf's head, rough but recognizable. He made it himself; I can see the marks of his claws in the grooves. He doesn't explain. Just sets it down and steps back.

Jace is next. A blade, small and sharp, tucked beside her hand. "For the road," he mutters. "In case she needs to fight her way wherever she's going."

Theo murmurs something I can't hear—a prayer, maybe, or a blessing—and leaves a sprig of dried herbs at her feet.

Wes places flowers at her shoulder. Doesn't speak. Doesn't need to.

Thane bows his head. Eyes closed. For a long moment, he's completely still—the ancient vampire king paying respect to a girl who tried to destroy everything he'd built. Then he steps back, face unreadable.

Seth goes next. He hesitates, hand hovering over the pyre. Then he places something small and dark beside her hand—a stone, smooth and black, worn from years of holding.

"I found it in the Void," he says quietly. "It was the only thing that kept me grounded. Reminded me there was something solid somewhere, even when everything else was smoke and shadow." He swallows. "She was there too. Trapped, like me. I think... I think she deserves something that survived."

My chest cracks.

Stellan is last.

He approaches the pyre slowly. Reaches out and places his palm flat over Riley's heart.

He stays like that for three heartbeats.

Then he withdraws, and his eyes meet mine.

"She was stronger than she knew," he says. "Most people are."

I nod. My throat is too tight for words.

Then Theo steps forward again. He holds something out to me—small, delicate, pulsing faintly with its own inner light.

A daisy.

The stem has that crystalline quality—delicate but strong, like glass spun from starlight. The petals shimmer with intricate swirling patterns, the same ones that marked the attic door back at the house. Back before I knew what any of it meant.

The same daisies I grew without meaning to, pushing up through floorboards while I slept. The ones that chimed like crystal wind chimes when the breeze caught them.

They grow wild in the sanctuary garden again. The Ether remembers what I made, even when I didn't know I was making it.

"You asked for one," Theo says quietly. "Earlier."

I did. I'd almost forgotten.

My hand shakes as I take it from him. The warmth spreads through my palm immediately—not burning but alive.

I step up to the pyre. Lean over Riley's still face, and tuck the daisy behind her ear. The crystalline petals catch against her dark hair, pulsing softly with light.

"You deserved flowers," I whisper. "Real ones. Ones that someone grew for you because they loved you."

The daisy glows brighter for just a moment. Like the Ether remembers her too.

I step back. Rhett is beside me. His hand finds mine, fingers lacing together.

"You ready?"

No. Not even close.

"Yes."

He lifts his other hand. Flame curls in his palm—warm, golden, steady. He's done this seventeen times this week. Practiced until he could control the heat, the spread, the way the fire catches and climbs.

But his hand is shaking.

I squeeze his fingers once. Let go.

He touches the pyre.

The fire catches immediately.

It races along the wooden beams, hungry and bright, climbing toward Riley's body. The heat pushes against my face, dries the tears I didn't realize were falling.

I watch her burn.

And then—

"Bree." Thane's voice is low. Strange. "Look."

I don't want to look away from the flames. From Riley. From the last physical proof that she existed.

But something in his tone makes me turn.

The Feeders are bowing. A ripple that starts at the front and spreads backward, hundreds of heads lowering in unison.

I don't understand. My brain won't process it.

"What are they—"

"They're not bowing to Riley." Stellan's hand tightens on mine. "They're bowing to you."

"They believe in what you're building," Thane says quietly.

The sob tears out of me before I can stop it.

These people—the people Riley enslaved, manipulated, broke—are bowing to me. Not because I demanded it. Not because I'm the Source, or the queen, or whatever the hell I'm supposed to be.

Because I showed up.

Because I asked for grace instead of vengeance.

Because I treated their dead with dignity, and now they're returning the favor.

My knees buckle.

Seth's hand slides into mine before I can fall. Gray presses his forehead to my shoulder. Wes wraps an arm around my waist, solid and grounding.

Theo anchors my other side. Rhett steps behind me, chest warm against my back. Thane's palm settles between my shoulder blades. Stellan's fingers cover mine where they grip Seth's hand.

They form a circle around me.

Holding me together while I fall apart.

The fire burns for a long time.

I watch until there's nothing left but ash and ember. Until the heat fades and the smoke thins and the stars start to peek through the darkening sky.

The Feeders drift away slowly. Quiet. Respectful. Some of them touch my shoulder as they pass—hesitant, like they're not sure they're allowed. Others just nod. A few are crying openly now, grief and relief and something harder all tangled together.

Zira stops in front of me. Her eyes are red.

"That was eighteen funerals in seven days," she says. "You showed up to every single one."

"They deserved witnesses."

"They did." She looks at the dying flames. "So did she."

I don't know what to say to that. So I just nod.

She squeezes my arm once and walks away.

Eventually, it's just us. Me and my men, standing in the cooling courtyard, watching the last of the flames die. I don't know how long we stay there.

Long enough for my tears to dry. Long enough for the ache in my chest to shift from sharp to dull. Long enough for something inside me to settle into a new shape.

I close my eyes and breathe.

Chapter 10
BREE

One year later.

One year.

I stand at the kitchen window, watching the sun set over a sanctuary that looks nothing like the ruin I first walked into years ago.

Houses dot the hillside now—dozens of them, nestled between the purple-leafed trees with their silver-veined bark. Smoke curls from chimneys. Children chase each other through the gardens, their laughter carrying on the evening breeze. The crystalline daisies catch the fading light, chiming softly as families make their way toward the main hall for dinner.

Four hundred and twelve people live here now.

I know because Theo keeps count. Updates me every morning over coffee, his notebook filled with names and needs and the endless logistics of running what has become, against all odds, a city.

"You're brooding."

Gray's voice comes from behind me. I don't turn.

"I'm reflecting. There's a difference."

"You've been reflecting at that window for twenty minutes." His hand settles on my hip, warm and grounding. "Mairen's going to come looking for you if you're late to your own dinner."

"It's not *my* dinner."

"It's absolutely your dinner. She's been cooking for three days."

I finally turn. Gray's watching me with those storm-gray eyes that see too much, always have. Behind him, the kitchen is chaos—Wes arguing with Jace about something, Rhett trying to keep Theo from reorganizing the spice cabinet, Seth quietly setting the table while everyone else creates disorder around him.

Thane and Stellan are conspicuously absent. Probably still getting ready. Thane takes longer with his appearance than I do, though he'd never admit it.

"One year," I say.

Gray's expression softens. "One year."

Since the battle. Since Riley. Since seventeen funerals and a blast that should have killed me and a choice I'm still not sure I understand.

Since I woke up surrounded by the people I love and realized I was finally, impossibly, home.

"Bree." Gray's thumb traces circles on my hip. "You're allowed to celebrate."

"I know."

"Do you?"

I meet his eyes. Hold them.

"I'm trying."

The dinner is chaos in the best possible way.

Mairen has outdone herself—the table groans under platters of roasted meat, fresh bread, vegetables that Rhett somehow didn't destroy. Candles float overhead, a trick Theo figured out three months ago and now deploys at every opportunity.

The seating happens naturally. Me at the center—always—with Seth on my right and Rhett on my left. Gray across from me, Wes beside him. Jace and Theo at the ends. Thane and Stellan anchoring the corners.

Mairen, Torn, and Kellan take the other side. Zira slides in late, as always, with zero apology.

"Traffic," she says when Jace raises an eyebrow.

"There's no traffic."

"Emotional traffic."

The food is perfect. The wine flows freely. Conversation overlaps and tangles—stories from the past year, jokes that only make sense if you were there, the easy rhythm of people who've become family.

I let it wash over me.

This is what we built. Not just the sanctuary, not just the houses and the gardens and the infrastructure. *This.* People gathered around a table, breaking bread, laughing at stupid jokes, belonging to each other.

A year ago, I didn't know if any of us would survive the night.

Now—

"Bree's crying," Jace announces.

"I am not."

"Your eyes are definitely wet."

"It's the candles. They're smoky."

"They're magical. They don't produce smoke."

"Then it's allergies."

"To what? Happiness?"

I throw a bread roll at his head. He catches it, grinning.

"Violence," he says. "At the dinner table. In front of the children."

"Kellan's sixteen."

"I meant Wes."

"Hey," Wes protests.

The table dissolves into laughter. Even Thane's mouth twitches.

Later, when the plates are cleared and Mairen's dessert has been demolished and the conversation has wound down to comfortable silence, I push back my chair.

"I want to show you something."

They follow me without question. Through the kitchen, out into the garden, past the crystalline daisies that chime as we pass. The path leads to the hill—the same overlook where we first saw the sanctuary when we came back from the Void. The highest point in the grounds, with a view that stretches for miles.

The sanctuary spreads below us like a living thing.

Lights flicker in windows. The training grounds where Rhett teaches fire control are empty now, but I can see the scorch marks from today's session. The library has grown three times the size since winter—Theo swears he's not doing it on purpose, but the Ether has opinions about his book collection.

Houses. Gardens. A fountain the Ether made two weeks ago, complete with fish that have strong feelings about water balloon fights.

A place where Feeders can exist without hiding. Where families can raise children without fear. Where magic and humanity tangle together into something new.

"Four hundred and twelve," I say softly.

"Four twenty-three, actually." Theo's voice is quiet. "Three new families arrived this afternoon."

I turn to look at them. My men. Arranged in a loose circle around me, faces lit by starlight and Ether-glow.

"When we first came here, this was ruins. Broken stone and dead gardens and a magic that had been sleeping for generations." I swallow. "Now look at it."

"You did this," Rhett says.

"*We* did this."

"You started it." Gray's voice is steady. "You woke it up. You made it possible."

I shake my head. "The Ether made it possible. And you. All of you." I look at Thane, at Stellan. "You didn't have to stay. After everything—the politics, the history, the fact that nothing bound you here—you stayed anyway."

Thane's silver eyes hold mine. "Where else would I go?"

"You had options."

"I had excuses." His voice is quiet. "There's a difference."

Stellan's mouth curves. "Besides. Someone has to keep you all from making terrible decisions."

"That's rich, coming from you," Jace mutters.

"I make *excellent* decisions. They just occasionally look terrible from the outside."

I laugh. It catches in my throat, turns into something bigger.

"I'm proud of what we built," I say. "All of it. The sanctuary, the families, the—" I gesture vaguely at the lights below. "Everything."

"But?" Wes prompts.

He knows me too well. They all do.

I take a breath.

"I haven't been back since before. Since the crown, since everything changed. And I think—" I stop. Try again. "I think I need to."

Understanding ripples through them. I see it in the way Gray goes still, the way Rhett's flame flickers between his fingers, the way Jace stops breathing for just a second.

"The house," Theo says slowly.

I nod.

The house. Where they lived together before any of this. Where I stumbled back into their lives bleeding and broken. Where the attic door appeared and the crown chose me and everything I thought I knew shattered into something new.

Where it all began.

"I want to go home."

The word hangs in the dark.

For a long moment, no one speaks.

Then Thane steps forward.

He moves with that ancient grace, the one that used to terrify me before I understood what it meant. His silver eyes hold mine as he crosses the distance between us.

And then he does something I've never seen him do.

He kneels.

Right there on the hillside, under the stars, the vampire who's lived for centuries and served on councils and played political games older than most civilizations—he kneels at my feet.

"Wherever you go," he says quietly, "I go."

My heart stops.

Stellan's laugh is soft, almost wondering. He steps forward too, but he doesn't kneel. Instead, he offers his hand—palm up, an invitation.

"If you're going home," he says, "then I'm already packed."

The others don't hesitate.

"Obviously we're coming," Gray says.

"Was that even a question?" Rhett's hand finds mine.

"Shotgun," Jace calls immediately.

"There's no shotgun. We're not—"

"There's always shotgun. It's a state of mind."

Seth just watches me with those quiet eyes. "You shouldn't go back alone."

Theo's already calculating. "We'll need to secure things here first. Make arrangements. But Mairen and Torn can handle most of it, and the infrastructure's stable enough—"

"Tomorrow," I say.

They all stop.

"Tomorrow, we leave."

I look at Thane, still kneeling. Reach down and take his hand, pull him to his feet.

Okay, okay, I tug and he stands on his own.

"All of us," I say. "Together."

The night holds the words.

And for the first time in a long time, I let myself think about where I came from. About going back to the beginning. About being whole enough, finally, to embrace it.

Chapter 11
BREE

I can't sleep.

I've tried everything. Counting Jace's snores—he's up to forty-seven. Mentally listing all the ways Gray's leg is cutting off circulation to my foot. Wondering if Wes knows he's drooling on my shoulder or if it's an unconscious talent he's perfected over time.

None of it works.

My brain keeps circling back to tomorrow. The house. The attic. The door with the swirling mark that started everything.

I give up around 3 AM.

Getting out of bed is its own challenge. Wes has basically fused himself to my left side. Gray's arm tightens when I try to slip free, some wolf instinct even in sleep that doesn't want to let me go. Rhett grumbles something that might be my name or might be a complaint about the temperature. Hard to tell.

It takes me five full minutes to extract myself without waking anyone. A new personal record.

I grab Rhett's hoodie from the chair—the sanctuary learned months ago to keep a rotation available—and slip into the hall.

The garden. I don't plan to go there. My feet just... do.

My daisies chime as I pass, catching moonlight. The trees are shadows against the sky. The air smells like jasmine and old magic and something that tugs at my chest.

The wall.

I stop walking.

Same stone. Same spot where Thane pressed me back and kissed me like I was worth something. Where I wrapped my legs around him and chose him and felt, for the first time in my life, like wanting didn't have to hurt.

My hand drifts to my throat before I can stop it. The bite mark healed months ago, but sometimes I swear I still feel it.

"Your thoughts are loud tonight."

I don't jump. My body knows him too well for that now.

Thane steps out from the shadow of the oak, pale in the moonlight. His shirt is half-buttoned, his hair loose around his shoulders. He looks like he dressed in a hurry to follow me.

He probably did.

"Couldn't sleep," I say.

"I noticed." He taps his chest once. "The bond."

Right. No secrets between us. Not the important ones.

"Sorry for waking you."

"You didn't." He moves closer, stops a few feet away. "I wasn't sleeping either."

We stand there, looking at each other. Looking at the wall.

"Last time we were here—" I start.

"You were terrified of me."

"I was terrified of everything." I cross my arms, the hoodie too big and smelling like Rhett's warmth. "You were just the scariest option available."

His mouth twitches. "And now?"

"Now you're maybe fourth. Fifth on a good day."

"I'm wounded."

"You'll recover."

Silence. But it's comfortable. The kind that happens when two people don't need to fill space with words.

"She won't bite, you know." A new voice, smooth and unhurried. "Though I suspect she'd let you if you asked nicely."

Stellan steps out from beneath the jasmine arch like he's been there all along. Probably has been. The bastard moves like smoke.

He's barefoot, wearing loose pants and nothing else. Moonlight catches the planes of his chest.

"How long have you been lurking?" I ask.

"Long enough to watch you two stare meaningfully at a wall." He stops beside Thane, hands sliding into his pockets. "Riveting stuff."

"We were having a moment."

"Were you? It looked more like mutual paralysis."

Thane makes a sound that might be a laugh. "Your timing is impeccable as always."

"I aim to displease." Stellan's gray eyes find mine. "The bond woke me too. You're practically vibrating with anxiety. And anticipation." He tilts his head, studying me. "Among other things."

Heat floods my face. "I'm not—"

"Your pulse says otherwise, darling."

"My pulse is none of your business."

"I'm an incubus. Your pulse is absolutely my business."

Thane pinches the bridge of his nose. "Must you?"

"Must I what? Be observant? Honest?"

"Insufferable. The word you're looking for is insufferable."

"That too."

I watch them—centuries of familiarity packed into every jab—and something loosens in my chest. This is what I needed. Not quiet contemplation. Not staring at walls. Just... this. Them. The easy rhythm of two people who've known each other long enough to skip the bullshit.

"So," I say, cutting through their verbal sparring. "Two ancient Feeders in a moonlit garden at 3 AM. What a coincidence."

They both go still. Predator-still.

Good.

"We weren't waiting," Thane says carefully.

"No?"

"We were... assessing."

"Discussing options," Stellan adds.

"Strategizing."

"About what?"

They exchange a glance. The kind of silent communication that drives me insane and they know it.

"You," Stellan says simply.

My whole body flushes. Not embarrassment—something lower, sharper.

"Oh," I manage.

Stellan's mouth curves. He definitely noticed.

"The night before you return home," he continues, moving closer. "The night before you face whatever's waiting there. We thought you might need distraction."

"Distraction."

"Support," Thane corrects.

"Comfort," Stellan counters.

"Very thorough comfort," Thane adds, and there's something in his voice that makes my knees unreliable.

"You two planned this."

"We discussed possibilities." Stellan stops close enough that I feel the warmth radiating off his skin. "Whether you take us up on any of them is entirely your choice."

Choice.

A year ago, I would have frozen. Would have doubted. Would have wondered what they really wanted.

That girl is gone.

Thank fuck.

I look at the wall behind me. At the stone where Thane first pressed me back and showed me what wanting could feel like.

Then I look at them. Two ancient, ridiculous creatures who've apparently been *discussing* me like I'm a project they're collaborating on.

"Full circle," I say quietly.

"Meaning?" Stellan asks.

"I was here two years ago. Scared and broken and convinced wanting too much would ruin everything." I take a breath. "And now I'm here again. And I know exactly what I want."

"Which is?"

I grab Stellan by the front of his pants and yank him forward.

The kiss isn't gentle. His mouth opens under mine immediately—no hesitation, no surprise—and he kisses me back with the kind of skill that comes from centuries of practice. His tongue slides against mine, tasting, taking, and I feel myself go liquid against him.

When I pull back, his eyes have gone dark.

"Well," he breathes. "That answers that."

Thane is watching with an expression I can't quite read. Hungry, yes. But something else. Something like satisfaction.

"Jealous?" I ask him.

"Hardly." He moves closer, crowding me between them. "I've been waiting for you to claim him for months."

"Claim him?"

"He's been yours since the night he climbed into your bed and let you sleep." Thane's voice drops lower. "You just hadn't decided to take him yet."

Stellan makes a sound—not quite a laugh. "He's not wrong."

"You two have definitely talked about this."

"At length," Stellan confirms. "In considerable detail."

"About *me*?"

"About how long it would take you to realize you could have whatever you wanted," Thane says. "And whether you'd ever actually ask for it."

The words hit somewhere deep. Because they're right. I've spent so long being afraid to want things. Afraid that needing too much would make everyone leave.

But they're still here. Both of them. Waiting for me to decide what happens next.

"The wall," I say.

Thane's eyes flash silver. "What about it?"

"That's where you first—" I stop, suddenly self-conscious.

"I remember." His voice drops into something rougher. "Every detail. The stone against your back. The sounds you made. The way you said my name when you came."

My breath catches.

"I've thought about it every night since," he continues, stepping closer until his chest brushes mine. "Wondered what it would feel like to take you there again. Properly. Without fear. Without rushing."

"And me?" Stellan's voice comes from behind me, close enough that I feel his breath on my neck. "Where do I fit in this?"

"Wherever she wants you."

The answer is instant. No jealousy. No competition. Just acknowledgment.

I turn to look at Stellan. "Is that true? You'd just let him have me?"

His smile is slow. "Darling, I'd watch him have you. And then I'd take my turn. And then, if you're very good, we might both have you at once." He pauses. "Unless that's too much?"

My thighs clench. Actually clench. Like my body is answering before my brain catches up.

"No," I say. "It's not too much."

"Then tell us what you want."

I look between them. Ancient. Dangerous. Mine.

"I want to stop thinking," I say. "Just for tonight. I want to feel something that isn't dread about tomorrow. I want both of you. However that works. Whatever that looks like."

The silence stretches.

Then Thane moves.

He's on me before I finish my next breath, hands gripping my hips, mouth claiming mine. The kiss is deep and filthy and exactly what I needed—his tongue stroking against mine, his teeth catching my bottom lip, his hands already sliding under the hoodie to find bare skin.

Stellan's hands find my waist from behind. His thumbs trace circles on my hip bones while Thane devours my mouth.

"May I?" he murmurs against my ear.

"Yes. You don't have to keep asking."

"I'll always ask." His fingers slip higher under the hoodie, skating across my ribs. "The first time, at least."

Thane's hands tighten on my hips. Stellan reads the shift instantly—steps aside like they've done this before, fluid and practiced—and then Thane is walking me backward until my shoulders hit the wall.

Same wall. Same stone. Everything different.

He breaks the kiss long enough to yank the hoodie over my head.

I'm not wearing a bra underneath—didn't see the point for a 3 AM existential crisis—and the night air raises goosebumps across my skin. Thane goes still, just for a heartbeat, looking at me.

"Still beautiful," he murmurs.

"Still weird when you stare."

"Get used to it." His hand comes up to cup my breast, thumb brushing over my nipple, and I gasp. "I plan to stare at you for the rest of my considerably long life."

Stellan moves in from the side, settling against the wall next to us, close enough to touch. His fingers trace down my arm, my hip, my thigh. "He's not wrong." His mouth finds my shoulder. "You're exquisite."

"You're both ridiculous."

"Possibly." Stellan's right hand slides lower, fingers tracing the waistband of my shorts. "But you like it."

I do. God help me, I really do.

Thane's mouth replaces his hand on my breast, tongue circling my nipple before he sucks it into his mouth. I arch into him, and Stellan's hands tighten on my hips, holding me steady.

"Patience," Stellan murmurs, turning me slightly so my back is against his chest. "We have all night."

"Maybe I don't want patience."

"What you want," Thane says against my skin, switching to my other breast, "is to be thoroughly taken care of. And that requires a certain amount of—" He bites down gently, and I cry out. "—attention to detail."

Stellan's fingers slip beneath my waistband. No underwear either—I really didn't think this through—and he finds out exactly how wet I am.

"She's ready," he observes, like he's commenting on the weather.

"Already?" Thane lifts his head, silver eyes catching mine. "We've barely started."

"What can I say." Stellan's fingers circle my clit, and my hips jerk. "She's responsive."

"Stop talking about me like I'm not here," I manage.

"Our apologies." Stellan slides one finger inside me, slow and deliberate, and my head falls back against his shoulder. "Is this better?"

"It's—" He adds a second finger, curling them just right, and I lose my words.

"Use your words, darling." His thumb finds my clit while his fingers work inside me. "Tell us what you want."

"I want—" Thane's mouth finds my nipple again, and between the two of them I can barely think. "I want more."

"More what?" Stellan's voice is patient, amused. "More fingers? More mouth? More—"

"More everything. Stop being so fucking controlled and just—"

Thane growls against my skin, actually growls, and suddenly his hands are on my shorts, yanking them down my legs. Stellan's fingers withdraw—I whimper at the loss—and then Thane is lifting me, pinning me against the wall with his hips, and I can feel how hard he is through his pants.

"Is this what you wanted?" His voice is rough, the careful control finally cracking. "Less patience?"

"Yes." I wrap my legs around his waist, grinding against him. "God, yes."

He reaches between us, freeing himself, and then he's pressing into me—slow, so slow, inch by inch until he's fully seated and I'm gasping against his shoulder.

"Still okay?" he asks, voice strained.

"If you ask me that one more time, I'm going to—"

He pulls out and slams back in, and the rest of my threat dissolves into a moan.

Stellan watches us from a few feet away, arms crossed, expression hungry but controlled. "Harder," he says. "She can take it."

Thane's hips snap forward, driving me into the wall, and I cry out. He does it again, and again, setting a rhythm that steals my breath.

"That's it." Stellan moves closer, one hand sliding into my hair, tilting my head back. "Look at you. Taking everything he gives you."

"Stellan—"

"Shh." He kisses me, soft and slow, a counterpoint to Thane's relentless pace. When he pulls back, his eyes are molten. "You're doing so well."

The praise hits something deep. My inner walls clench around Thane, and he groans.

"She liked that," Thane manages.

"I noticed." Stellan's hand slides down between us, finding where Thane and I are joined, and his fingers find my clit. "Let's see what else she likes."

The dual sensation—Thane driving into me while Stellan's fingers work my clit—is overwhelming. I'm caught between them, unable to do anything but feel.

"She's close," Stellan observes.

"I can feel it." Thane shifts his angle, hitting something deeper, and I see stars. "There?"

"*There.*"

"Excellent."

Stellan's fingers speed up, matching Thane's rhythm, and I'm climbing fast, too fast—

"Not yet." Stellan's hand stills, and I sob in frustration.

"What—why—"

"Because I want to watch you break." His voice is pure silk. "And you're not quite there yet."

"I hate you."

"No, you don't." He kisses my jaw, my throat, the spot just below my ear. "You love that we know exactly how to take you apart."

Thane slows his pace, rolling his hips instead of thrusting, keeping me on the edge without letting me fall. "Tell us what you need."

"I need to come," I grit out. "Please."

"Please what?" Stellan's fingers trace circles around my clit, never quite giving me enough pressure.

"Please let me come. Please. I'll do anything—"

Thane and Stellan exchange a glance over my shoulder.

Then they both move at once.

Thane drives into me hard, hitting that perfect spot, while Stellan's fingers press down on my clit hard. The orgasm crashes through me like a wave, my whole body shaking, Thane's name and Stellan's name tangling together on my tongue.

Thane follows moments later, groaning against my throat as he spills inside me. His fangs graze my pulse.

"Yes," I breathe before he can ask. "Do it."

He bites.

The pain transforms instantly, flooding my system with something deeper than pleasure. The bond flares, his satisfaction and my surrender tangling together. The feeding isn't taking—it's completing. A circuit finally closed.

The bite pushes me into another peak, smaller but sharper, and I clench around him as he feeds.

When he withdraws, sealing the wound with his tongue, I'm boneless.

"Holy shit," I say intelligently.

"Indeed." Stellan is still hard, still patient, watching us with dark eyes. "When you've recovered, I believe it's my turn."

Thane eases out of me, and before my legs can give out entirely, Stellan is there—taking my weight from Thane, pulling me back against his chest.

"The grass," I manage. "My back is complaining about the wall."

"How romantic." But he's already lifting me, one arm under my knees, carrying me toward the soft grass beneath the oak tree.

He lowers me down gently, then stands back to strip off his pants. In the moonlight, he's all elegant lines and lean muscle, and when he settles between my thighs, I can feel how hard he is against my hip.

"Any requests?" he asks, like we're ordering dinner.

"Surprise me."

His mouth curves. "Dangerous words."

He starts at my throat, kissing down my body with agonizing slowness. Collarbone. The swell of my breasts. My nipples, already sensitive from Thane's attention. My stomach. My hip bones.

"Stellan—"

"Patience." He settles between my legs, breath warm against my inner thigh. "I want to taste you first."

His mouth finds me, and I nearly come off the ground.

He eats me out like he has all the time in the world, tongue tracing patterns I can't follow, lips and teeth adding just enough edge. When he slides two fingers inside me, I'm already shaking.

"Still so wet," he murmurs against my skin. "Even after Thane filled you. Is that for me, darling?"

"Yes. God, yes."

"Good."

He adds a third finger, stretching me, and his tongue finds my clit. The combination is devastating. I'm climbing again, faster than I expected—

And then he stops.

"Stellan," I groan. "I swear to god—"

"You already came twice." He kisses my inner thigh, maddeningly gentle. "The third one, you earn."

"How?"

He prowls up my body, covering me, the head of his cock pressing against my entrance. "By asking nicely."

I grab his hair and yank him down to my mouth. "Fuck me," I say against his lips. "Please."

He slides inside me in one long stroke, and we both groan.

He's different from Thane. Where Thane is intensity and claim, Stellan is precision and patience. He sets a slow rhythm, deep and deliberate, watching my face for every reaction.

And then I feel it—his power.

Not a push. Not an intrusion. Just... quiet. The anxious chatter in my brain goes silent. Tomorrow disappears. The attic, the door, the ghosts—gone. There's nothing left but sensation. His body moving in mine. The cool grass against my back. The pleasure building low in my belly.

"There she is," Stellan murmurs. "Just us now. Nothing else."

I can't think. Don't want to think. Just feel.

Thane settles beside us, and his hands find my wrists, drawing them up over my head, pinning them gently to the grass. The stretch changes the angle of everything, and I moan.

"Hold still," Thane says. "Let him work."

Stellan's rhythm deepens. His power pulses through me in waves, and every thrust feels amplified—pleasure layered on pleasure until I can't tell where one sensation ends and another begins.

"More," I gasp. "Please, more—"

"Greedy." But Stellan shifts his angle, and I nearly come off the ground. "There?"

"*There.*"

His pace builds. Thane's grip tightens on my wrists, keeping me anchored while Stellan drives into me. The pressure coils tighter, deeper than before—something I don't recognize building at my core.

"There it is," Stellan breathes. "That's what I was looking for."

Thane releases one of my wrists, brings my hand to his mouth. His lips close around two of my fingers, sucking gently, and the unexpected sensation sends sparks down my spine.

"Oh god—"

Stellan's power surges. My mind empties completely—nothing but them, nothing but this, nothing but the pleasure cresting impossibly high—

"Let go," Stellan breathes. "I want to feel you."

I shatter.

Not like before. This is different—deeper, wetter. I feel myself clench around him and then release, and there's a rush of liquid heat between us that I've never—

"*Fuck*," Stellan groans, and his hips stutter. "Did you just—"

I can't answer. I'm still coming, still clenching, still gushing around him as he drives into me one last time and follows me over the edge.

He collapses half on top of me, breathing hard. Thane releases my other wrist, and my arms fall boneless to the grass.

"That was—" Stellan starts.

"New," I manage. "That was new."

"You've never—"

"No."

Thane's hand finds mine, fingers interlacing. "Incubus," he says, like that explains everything.

Maybe it does.

We lie there in the grass, tangled together, all three of us. The sky is starting to lighten.

"Full circle," I murmur.

Thane's thumb traces circles on the back of my hand. "Hmm?"

"When we first got here, I was scared and convinced I was too damaged for anyone to want." I stare up at the fading stars. "And now I feel…"

"What?" Stellan asks softly, shifting to lie beside me.

"Ready." The word surprises me with how true it is. "I feel ready."

Tomorrow I go home. Tomorrow I face the attic and the door and every ghost I left behind.

But tonight, I'm exactly where I want to be.

"Thank you," I whisper. "Both of you."

"For what?" Thane props himself up on one elbow, looking down at me.

"For the really excellent distraction." I laugh. "For figuring out how to share without killing each other."

"It's a delicate balance," Stellan says. "But you're worth the effort."

"That's the nicest thing you've ever said to me."

"Don't get used to it. I have a reputation to uphold."

Thane snorts. "What reputation? You've been disgustingly soft since you met her."

"I have not—"

"You climbed into her bed to help her sleep. *Feeding.* Without asking for anything."

Stellan is quiet. "That was different."

"Was it?"

"Yes." His voice drops lower. "That was before I realized I'd do anything she asked."

Something warm blooms in my chest.

When dawn finally breaks, they help me to my feet. My legs are shaky. My neck throbs where Thane bit. I'm definitely going to walk funny for the rest of the day.

I'm okay with that.

Chapter 12
GRAY

Bree moves through the sanctuary like she's memorizing it.

Slowly. Deliberately. Her fingers trail along the stone walls as she walks, her eyes lingering on doorways and windows and the small details that have accumulated in our time here. The reading nook Theo claimed. The scorch marks Rhett left on the kitchen ceiling. The spot by the fountain where Jace nearly drowned himself trying to impress her.

I hang back, watching. That's my job. Has been since long before I knew what I was.

She's different this morning. Still Bree—still the woman who woke up tangled between Thane and Stellan on the grass, still the woman who limped back to bed with a satisfied smile and fell asleep for another three hours next to me. But something's shifted.

She's not bracing.

That's what catches me. The old Bree braced for everything—touch, kindness, change. This Bree walks through goodbyes like someone who expects to come back.

Zira finds us in the main hall, arms crossed, expression carefully blank. She's not fooling anyone.

"So," Zira says. "You're actually doing this."

"I'm actually doing this."

"Stupid."

"Probably."

They stare at each other. Zira breaks first, pulling Bree into a hug that's more tackle than embrace.

"My room," Bree says against her shoulder. "Use it while I'm gone. The bed's ridiculous and the bathtub could fit six people."

"I know. I helped you test that theory."

Bree laughs. Zira doesn't let go.

"You don't have to stay here to be ours," Zira says, quiet enough that I almost miss it. "You know that, right?"

"I know."

"Good." Zira pulls back, her usual sharpness sliding back into place. "Now get out of here before I say something embarrassing."

Bree's already moved on before Zira's mask fully settles. But I see it slip. Just for a second.

I file it away. Keep walking.

Mairen's waiting in the kitchen, because of course she is. The woman has some kind of sixth sense for departures. The counter is covered in wrapped packages—food for the road, enough to feed an army for a week.

"You'll eat," Mairen says. Not a question.

"I'll eat."

"And you'll sleep. Properly. Not whatever you call sleep when you're running yourself into the ground."

"I'll try."

Mairen's hands flutter—adjusting a package, smoothing a napkin, finding reasons to keep moving. Then she stops. Looks at Bree with something raw in her eyes.

"When we came here," she says slowly, "I thought we were following power. A queen. Something to kneel to." She shakes her head. "But that's not what you gave us. You gave us a home. A real one."

Bree's throat works.

"And now you can leave," Mairen continues. "You can go back to wherever you came from, and this place will still be standing when you get back. That's how I know you did it right."

I watch Bree's shoulders loosen. Watch the tension she didn't know she was carrying drain away.

"Thank you," Bree whispers. "For everything."

"Thank me by eating the sandwiches."

The council chamber is our last stop.

Not the old one—not the Council of Five with their ancient thrones and power plays. This is something Bree built. A round room off the main hall, added six months ago when the sanctuary's population selected leaders outgrew informal kitchen-table decisions.

It's not what I expected when she first proposed it. More seats than I can count, arranged in concentric circles. Feeders and shifters and seers and elementals, all of them present. All of them watching Bree with something that isn't fear.

She doesn't speak much. Listens while they report—supply lines, ward maintenance, a territorial dispute between two shifter families that got resolved without bloodshed. Routine stuff. The machinery of a community running itself.

When it's over, she stands. Nods once.

That's it.

No speeches. No grand proclamations. She just walks out, and the council keeps meeting without her.

I follow, something settling in my chest.

This place doesn't need her anymore. Not to survive.

And that's exactly why she can leave.

The cars are loaded by the time we make it outside. Two vehicles—Thane, Stellan, Seth and Theo taking one; the rest of us piling into the other.

Jace is already bitching about seating arrangements.

"I'm not sitting in the middle again. I have long legs. It's a medical condition."

"Your medical condition is being a pain in the ass," Wes says, shoving him toward the back seat.

"That's not a recognized diagnosis."

"I'll recognize my fist in your face."

"Kinky."

Rhett claims the driver's seat without discussion. His car, his grandmother's house we're driving to. None of us argue.

"Give me a minute." I say and Rhett nods.

I do a final perimeter sweep. Not because I think anything's wrong. Just because that's what I do.

The sanctuary hums under my feet. Steady. Alive. Safe.

I mark it in my mind. *This is secure. This will be here when we come back.*

Then I get in the car—back seat, Bree in the middle, Jace crammed against the other window despite his complaints. Wes rides shotgun.

The drive is quiet at first. The kind of silence that happens when no one knows what to say.

I felt the magic thin the moment we crossed the sanctuary boundary—that familiar ache of the world going flat and ordinary. We've been driving through nothing for hours now. Just highway, just asphalt, just the kind of mundane landscape that has no idea magic exists.

Bree stares out the window, watching it pass.

Her heartbeat is steady through the bond. Not calm, exactly. But not panicked either.

She's not afraid.

She's bracing.

Different thing.

Jace breaks first, because Jace always breaks first.

"So," he says, "anyone want to play I Spy? I spy with my little eye, something boring as fuck."

"The road," Wes says flatly.

"The road! Damn, you're good at this."

"I will turn this car around," Rhett warns.

"You won't."

"Try me."

I sigh. "Can we have five minutes of peace?"

"Peace is overrated. Peace is what happens when interesting people aren't around."

The bickering washes over me. Familiar. Grounding. Mile by mile, the tension in the car loosens. Not gone—just manageable.

Bree's still watching out the window. But her mouth twitches when Jace starts singing off-key, and she doesn't hide it.

"I should warn you," Jace says, leaning forward between the front seats, "the place is probably a disaster. Two years of nobody living there? Cobwebs. Dead mice. Possibly a raccoon family that's claimed squatter's rights."

"Sorry, man." Wes glances at Rhett. "Your grandmother's place, just sitting there rotting. That sucks."

Rhett's quiet for a moment. His hands flex on the steering wheel.

"It's not rotting."

"What?"

"Thane and Stellan sent people. Last month." He keeps his eyes on the road. "Cleaners. Landscapers. Someone to check the pipes and roof. The whole place has been aired out, restocked. It's ready."

Silence.

"They did what?" Bree asks softly.

"They wanted you to come back to what you remembered." Rhett shrugs, but I catch the tension in his shoulders. The gratitude he doesn't know how to voice. "Not ruins."

I didn't know that. None of us did. Thane and Stellan just... handled it. Quietly. Without asking for credit.

"That's..." Jace trails off for once. "Actually kind of sweet. In a creepy, centuries-old-money kind of way."

"Stellan's an incubus, not a vampire," Wes says.

"Creepy ancient incubus money. Same energy."

Bree doesn't say anything. But her hand reaches forward, finds Rhett's shoulder, squeezes once.

He clears his throat. Doesn't shake her off.

We turn onto a quiet street. Ordinary houses. Ordinary lawns. The kind of neighborhood where nothing magical ever happens.

Except something did.

The house sits at the end of the block. And Rhett was right—it's not the shambles I expected. The lawn is trimmed. The paint looks fresh. The windows are clean, curtains pulled back to let in light.

It looks like someone lives here. Like someone's been taking care of it.

Because someone has.

Rhett pulls up to the curb. Cuts the engine.

No one moves.

Bree stares at the house through the windshield. Her jaw is tight, but her breathing is even.

"Your grandmother," I say quietly. "She'd be glad it's being used again."

Rhett's hands tighten on the steering wheel. "Yeah." His voice is rough. "She would."

The second car pulls up behind us. Doors open, close. Footsteps on pavement.

Still, none of us move to get out.

The house waits. Patient. Ordinary.

It has no idea what's coming back to it.

Chapter 13
BREE

The car door opens, and I step out before anyone can tell me to wait.

The house looks exactly the same.

Same faded blue paint—fresh coat, but they matched the color. Same lace curtains in the windows. The lawn is trimmed, the walkway swept, but it's still the same cracked concrete Jace trips over every time.

Thane and Stellan's work. Making sure I came back to memory, not ruin.

I stand on the sidewalk, staring.

"It's unlocked," Rhett says quietly behind me. "Thane made sure."

"You want us to go first?" Jace offers. "Sweep for ghosts? I'm very brave, you know. Incredibly brave. Some would say foolishly—"

"Jace." Wes's voice is gentle. "Shut up."

I barely hear them.

The house waits.

I step forward.

No one stops me.

The door swings open easily, and I'm hit with the smell of old wood and lemon soap. And underneath that—them. All of them. It smells like the first night I came here, terrified and shaking in Rhett's borrowed clothes. It smells like the mornings Jace made pancakes while the others pretended not to hover. It smells like home.

The interior looks exactly right. Furniture where it should be. Light falling the same way through the same windows. No dust, no decay.

The guys file in behind me, footsteps quiet. Even Jace doesn't speak. They move through the space carefully, like they know this moment isn't theirs to claim.

I don't stop in the living room, where Wes caught me trying to leave that first morning. Don't pause at the kitchen doorway, where Gray told me I wasn't a burden. Don't linger at the bottom of the stairs, where I used to hesitate before going up to the room they gave me.

I just walk.

Up the stairs. Down the hall. To the attic.

Gray realizes where I'm going before anyone else does. I feel it through the bond—not alarm, just recognition.

No one speaks.

They follow.

The attic looks the same. Window seat where I used to curl up at dawn. Mismatched furniture they brought up piece by piece. Soft gray walls. The space they built for me before I ever knew I needed it.

But my eyes go straight to the door.

The door that shouldn't exist. The door that called to me even before I understood why.

I stop in front of it.

The sigil has changed.

It's not the old symbol. Not the one that made the mist stir and whisper when I first touched it.

This is mine.

The same sigil that bloomed in the sanctuary when I took my oath. The same pattern etched into Ether and stone and the scars I chose to give. Silver lines on dark wood.

It's not burning.

It's not shifting.

It's just... there. Waiting.

I smile. Small. Real.

My hand reaches out before I decide to move it. The wood is warm under my fingers. The sigil pulses once, and the door swings open.

Soft light spills out. The room beyond shouldn't exist—the attic isn't big enough to hold it. But it's there, ancient stones and impossible space, just like before.

And at the center—

The crown.

Sitting on a pedestal of pale gold light. Not looming. Not demanding. Not doing anything, really.

Just waiting.

For me.

I stand in the doorway. The crown gleams softly. It doesn't call to me. Doesn't pull. It's just there, and I'm here, and the space between us is mine to cross.

Or not.

I take a breath.

And I close the door.

The click is soft. Not forever—just for now.

I turn around.

They're all watching me. Not the door. Not the sigil.

Me.

The crown can wait. For the first time in my life, I'm done putting myself last.

"I might be queen," I say. It comes out calm. Simple. "But I'm choosing to be happy first." I look at each of them. "And I'm forever yours."

No one kneels. No one rushes forward. The silence stretches—but it's not empty.

Gray speaks first. "Good."

One word. That's all he needs.

Rhett's voice is rough. "About damn time."

Wes steps closer, eyes bright. "You know we'd have waited forever, right? However long it took you to choose yourself."

"Longer," Jace says. And for once, there's no joke underneath it. Just truth.

Thane inclines his head—the barest movement, but from him it's everything. "My queen chooses herself. As she should."

"Took you long enough," Stellan murmurs. But his eyes are warm. "Welcome home, darling."

Seth doesn't say anything for a moment—just looks at me like he's memorizing this. "You're the first person who ever made me believe I could choose too," he says quietly. "Thank you."

And then Theo. He steps forward, takes my hand, and his voice is steady. Certain. The same voice that found me in the dark all those years ago.

"You don't have to be perfect to be worthy of being seen," he says. "I told you that once. Do you remember?"

My throat tightens. "I remember."

"We always saw you, Bree." His thumb brushes across my knuckles. "But now... now you see yourself."

The bond hums between us. All of them. All of me.

And for the first time since I was seven years old, I'm not afraid of what comes next.

THE END...

BONUS CHAPTER

You survived five books of chaos, near-death experiences, and emotional devastation.
The least I can do is let you watch them be deliriously happy. Among other things.
(This is me winking at you.)

BONUS: BREE

Four years later

The retreat is already loud when I push open the door.

Not waiting-for-me loud. Tuesday loud. The kind of noise that happens when eight people have stopped being careful around each other and just exist—overlapping conversations, someone's music playing low, the clink of glasses, laughter that keeps interrupting itself.

Four years of this, and I still pause in the doorway sometimes. Not because it's fragile. Because it's not.

I take in the room in pieces:

Gray and Wes on the long couch, Wes draped across Gray's lap like he's furniture. Gray's hand rests on the back of his neck—not gripping, just there. Wes keeps interjecting into some conversation across the room, and each time he does, Gray's fingers tighten briefly—a warning—before releasing. Casual. Familiar.

Jace is on the floor near the fireplace, ostensibly playing cards with Stellan, except neither of them is looking at their hands. Jace says something—I catch the tail end, something filthy wrapped in a joke—and Stellan's mouth twitches. Not the distant amusement he used to wear like armor. Something warmer. He flicks a card at Jace's head, and Jace catches it, grinning.

That's new. Or not new—*newer*. I've watched them circle each other for the past year, Stellan's elegance meeting Jace's chaos and finding something unexpected there. They haven't done anything about it. Or maybe they have and I missed it. Either way, the comfort between them has weight now.

Theo is in the armchair by the window with a book, except his eyes aren't on the pages. They're tracking the room the way they always do—Wes's body language, the tension in Rhett's shoulders, the angle of Jace's smile. He's not reading. He's holding. Grounding the space just by being in it.

Thane, Seth, and Rhett are at the bar in the corner, and that's the thing that makes me smile.

Thane and Seth couldn't be in the same room without circling each other like threats once. Now Seth is leaning against the counter, drink in hand, while Rhett explains something with increasingly emphatic gestures. Thane's expression is caught between genuine confusion and aristocratic disdain. Seth laughs at something, and Thane looks almost offended, then reluctantly amused.

No one has noticed me yet.

I could announce myself. Could walk in and let the energy shift around me the way it used to, everyone recalibrating to my presence like I'm the axis everything turns on.

Instead, I just... join.

Seth sees me first.

Not because he was watching the door—because he feels me. The bond, or just years of learning my rhythms. His eyes find mine across the room and his face does something soft and warm before he's already moving.

He meets me halfway, drink abandoned on the bar, and his hands find my waist like they belong there.

"Kids down?"

"Both lights green." I lean into him, let his warmth sink in. "Aiden tried to convince me there was a monster in his closet that required immediate investigation."

"Was there?"

"It was his shoes. He threw them in there this morning and forgot."

Seth's laugh rumbles through his chest. "Terrifying."

"He was very brave about it."

His mouth brushes my temple, then my cheekbone, then the corner of my lips. Not a kiss yet—a hello.

"Come on," he says, tugging me toward the couch. "Rhett's trying to explain fantasy football to Thane and it's the funniest thing I've seen all week."

The couch is a sprawl.

Gray hasn't moved Wes from his lap, just shifted to make room, and Wes's head is pillowed on his thigh now while Gray's fingers card through his hair. Rhett is mid-sentence, something about point spreads.

"—so you're telling me," Thane says slowly, "that you spend actual currency to pretend you own athletes who then perform for imaginary points."

"It's not pretend ownership, it's—"

"It's absolutely pretend ownership," Jace calls from the floor. "That's the whole point."

"You're not helping," Rhett says.

"I'm never helping. You should know this by now."

Seth pulls me down onto the couch, and I end up half in his lap, legs draped over Wes's calves. Wes makes a sleepy sound of acknowledgment, reaches down to pat my ankle without opening his eyes.

"Hi, Bree."

"Hi, Wes."

"Gray's being mean to me."

"I'm petting your hair," Gray says mildly.

"Meanly."

Gray tugs—just slightly, just enough to make Wes's breath catch—and then resumes the gentle stroking. "Better?"

"...yes."

Rhett has given up on explaining fantasy football. He's watching Gray and Wes instead, and I recognize that look—heat banked behind careful observation. Rhett likes to see. Likes to understand exactly what's happening before he decides whether to join.

"You're staring," I tell him.

"I'm appreciating."

"Voyeur."

"Absolutely." He doesn't even pretend to be ashamed anymore. "You're one to talk. I saw you in the doorway."

"I was taking in the room."

"You were watching Stellan look at Jace."

Shit. He clocked that?

"I don't know what you're talking about."

Rhett's grin is slow and knowing. "Sure you don't."

The energy shifts without anyone announcing it.

Theo sets his book aside. Stellan's card game with Jace has devolved into Jace trying to build a tower out of the deck while Stellan watches with an expression that's either fondness or exasperation. Thane has gone quiet, his attention sharpening the way it does when he's thinking about something he wants.

Gray's hand has migrated. Still in Wes's hair, but lower now, fingers brushing the nape of his neck in a way that makes Wes shift restlessly.

"You're squirming," Gray observes.

"You're teasing."

"I'm barely touching you."

"You're *barely touching me* in a very specific way."

I feel Seth's chest shake with silent laughter behind me. His hand has found its way under my shirt—when did that happen?—palm warm against my stomach.

"You cold?" he murmurs against my ear.

"No."

"Then why are you shivering?"

Because his fingers are tracing patterns just above my waistband. Because Gray is telling Wes to hold still in *that* voice. Because Theo has stopped pretending to read and is watching all of us with eyes that see too much.

"Just feeling things," I say.

"Good things?"

"The best things."

Jace's card tower collapses. He swears loudly, which makes Stellan laugh—actually laugh, not the polished chuckle he deploys at dinner parties—and Jace's head whips around to stare at him.

"Did you just—"

"It was amusing."

"You *laughed*. Stellan laughed. Someone mark the calendar."

"I laugh."

"You make sounds that technically qualify as laughter. That was different." Jace is grinning now, delighted. "That was a real laugh. I'm counting that as a win."

"It's not a competition."

"Everything's a competition. I'm winning."

Stellan rolls his eyes, but he's still smiling. And when Jace leans over to gather his scattered cards, Stellan's hand brushes his shoulder. Casual. Brief. The kind of touch that could be accidental if you weren't paying attention.

Jace goes still for just a second. Then keeps moving, keeps talking, but there's a flush creeping up the back of his neck.

Yeah. There's definitely something there.

Things start overlapping.

That's the only way to describe it—the room stops being separate conversations and starts being one continuous thing. Rhett moves to the floor near the fireplace, and Jace immediately lays down next to him, complaining about card-tower sabotage. Gray pulls Wes upright and into a kiss that goes deep fast, and Wes makes a sound against his mouth that I feel in my own chest.

Theo rises from his chair.

The room notices. It's subtle—a shift in attention, everyone tracking his movement without looking directly at him. Four years ago, Theo had to ask for attention. Had to earn the space to speak. Now he just takes it.

He crosses to the couch, and the crowd parts for him without being asked. Gray and Wes break their kiss but don't separate, making room. Rhett shifts Jace's weight. Seth's arms tighten around me.

Theo stops in front of us. Looks down at me with those quiet, certain eyes.

"Come here," he says.

It's not a question. Not a request. Just a statement of what's going to happen.

I go.

Theo takes me to the bedroom that branches off the main space.

Not to separate us—the door stays open, the sounds of the others filtering through. Just to have me for a minute. To focus without distraction.

"You've been stretched thin all day," he says, pressing me back against the wall. "I could feel it."

"Kids. Sanctuary stuff. The delegation from the Council."

"I know." His hands frame my face, thumbs brushing my cheekbones. "I'm not asking you to explain. I'm telling you to stop carrying it."

"I'm fine—"

"Bree." His voice is gentle but immovable. "Put it down."

This is what Theo does now. Sees the weight I'm holding and tells me—doesn't ask, *tells* me—to let go of it. Four years ago, I would have argued. Would have insisted I could handle it, that I didn't need help.

Now I just... exhale.

The tension drains out of my shoulders. He watches it go, nodding slowly, and then his mouth is on mine.

Theo kisses like he does everything else—patient and thorough and completely unhurried. Like he has all the time in the world to take me apart and every intention of doing exactly that. His thigh presses between my legs and I rock against it without thinking, chasing friction, already desperate for more.

"There it is," he murmurs against my lips. "That's what I wanted. Stop thinking."

"Hard to think when you—*ah*—"

His hands slide down my body, stripping me efficiently—dress over my head, bra unhooked, panties pushed down until I'm bare against the wall and he's still fully clothed. The power imbalance shouldn't be hot, but god, it is.

"All day," he says, dropping to his knees in front of me, "I've been thinking about this."

"About—about what?"

"Getting you alone." He lifts my thigh over his shoulder, spreading me open. "Making you come on my tongue before you go back out there." His breath is warm against my cunt. "Sending you back to them shaking, so they know exactly who had you first."

"That's—fuck—that's possessive."

"Is it?" He doesn't wait for an answer. His mouth finds me, tongue dragging through my folds, and I nearly slam my head back against the wall.

Theo.

He eats pussy like it's communion—reverent and thorough and absolutely devastating. His tongue circles my clit before dipping inside me, tasting me, he's already learned what makes me twitch. Two fingers push in, crooking against that spot that makes my legs shake, and I fist my hands in his hair.

"Theo—" I'm already close, embarrassingly fast. "I'm going to—"

"Good." He sucks my clit into his mouth and *hums*, and I shatter.

The orgasm rips through me, my whole body convulsing, my pussy clenching around his fingers. He works me through it, gentling but not stopping, and before I can catch my breath, he's building me up again.

"One more," he says against me. "I want one more."

"I can't—"

"You can." His fingers twist, hitting that spot again, and I keen. "You're going to give me one more, and then I'm going to walk you back out there so fucked out that everyone knows what I did to you."

Gods.

This is Theo now—four years of learning exactly how to take me apart, exactly what I need. He knows when to push and when to back off, when to be gentle and when to make me *earn* it.

He backs off now, slowing his fingers, letting the wave recede. I whimper.

"Please—"

"Not yet." His tongue traces lazy circles around my clit, never quite touching it. "Tell me what you want."

"I want to come. Please, Theo, I need—"

"I know what you need." He presses a kiss to my inner thigh, almost chaste, while his fingers keep their maddening rhythm. "I always know. But I want to hear you say it."

"I want your mouth on my clit," I gasp. "I want you to make me come. Please, please—"

He rewards me.

His mouth seals over my clit and he sucks *hard*, fingers driving into me, and I scream. The second orgasm hits even harder than the first, waves and waves of pleasure crashing through me until I'm boneless, held up only by the wall and Theo's hands on my hips.

When he finally pulls back, his face is wet with me. He looks *satisfied*.

"That's what I needed," he says, pressing one more kiss to my oversensitive clit—making me jerk—before rising to his feet. "Now you're ready."

I can barely stand. "Ready for what?"

His smile is quiet and certain. "For whatever comes next."

I'm still shaking when he leads me back to the main room.

Things have progressed.

Gray has Wes bent over the arm of the couch, fucking into him with long slow strokes. Wes's face is pressed into the cushions, hands gripping the fabric, making sounds that are barely human. I can see where they're connected—Gray's thick cock disappearing into Wes's body over and over, slick and obscene.

My cunt clenches at the sight. Four years, and watching them together still does this to me—makes my mouth go dry, makes heat pool low in my belly. The way Gray holds Wes down, the way Wes *takes* it, the sounds he makes like he's being ruined in the best possible way.

Gray's eyes find mine like he knows. His gaze drags down my naked body—flushed skin, trembling thighs, the evidence of what Theo did to me probably written all over my face—and his rhythm doesn't falter. If anything, it deepens. He reaches out with one hand, catches my wrist, pulls me close enough to kiss.

"Good?" he murmurs against my mouth.

"Very."

His thumb strokes my pulse point once, twice, then releases me. Back to Wes. But his eyes stay on mine for another beat, dark with promise. *Later.*

Rhett is sprawled in the armchair near the fireplace, legs spread, watching the room like he's memorizing it. He's hard—I can see the thick line of his cock straining against his jeans—but his hands stay loose on the armrests. Deliberate restraint. He catches me looking and his mouth curves. *Best view in the house,* that smile says.

Stellan is on the couch near Wes's head, fingers carding through his hair, entirely focused on the man beneath him. He's already shirtless, pale skin gleaming in the low light, and the hard line of his cock presses against his slacks. Patient. Hungry. *Waiting* for Gray to finish so he can take his turn.

Thane and Seth have migrated to the other end of the room, and Seth catches my eye when I walk in—grins, crooks a finger. *Come here when you're ready.*

But before I can move, Jace moves beside me.

"Hey, beautiful." His grin is wicked. "Theo have fun with you?"

"I—yes—"

"Good." His hand slides around my waist, pulling me back against his chest. "Now it's my turn to play."

"Jace, I want to watch—"

"So watch." His mouth finds my ear, his breath hot against my skin. "I'm not stopping you."

His hand slides down my stomach, slipping between my thighs, and I gasp. I'm still swollen and sensitive from Theo, and Jace's fingers find my clit with unerring accuracy.

"Eyes on them," he murmurs. "Watch what Gray does to Wes. I want to feel you react."

Gray's rhythm is faltering, and I know what that means. I try to focus on them even as Jace's fingers circle my clit in slow, maddening strokes.

"Wes," Gray grits out, fingers digging into Wes's hips hard enough to bruise. "I'm—"

"Do it," Wes gasps. "Please, I need—"

Gray slams in one final time and holds, burying himself to the hilt as he comes. I watch his cock pulse, watch Wes's hole clench around him, milking every drop—and Jace chooses that exact moment to push two fingers inside me.

I moan, knees buckling, and Jace laughs against my neck.

"That's it. Keep watching."

Wes shudders beneath Gray but doesn't come—his own cock hangs heavy and leaking between his legs, untouched, desperate.

"Good boy." Gray pulls out slowly, and I can see his come starting to drip from Wes's fucked-open hole. "You held on for me."

"Gray—" Wes's voice cracks with need. "I need—I can't—"

"I know." Gray steps back, and his eyes find Stellan's. Something passes between them—permission, invitation, recognition. "He needs more than I can give him right now."

Jace's fingers curl inside me, hitting that spot that makes stars burst behind my eyes. I whimper, trying to keep my focus on the couch, on Stellan's smirk he can't hide.

"You're so wet," Jace murmurs. "Is that from Theo? Or from watching them?"

"Both," I manage. "Gods, Jace—"

"Shh. Watch."

Stellan rises from the couch, and I see him clearly for the first time tonight. He's stripped down to his pants, pale elegant muscle on display. When he undoes his belt, his cock springs free—long and curved and flushed dark with want.

Wes makes a sound just *looking* at it. So do I—though mine comes out strangled because Jace has added a third finger and I'm stretched and full and trying desperately to pay attention to what's happening on the couch.

"Four years," Stellan murmurs, moving behind Wes, trailing his fingers down that sweat-slicked spine. "Four years of watching you. Wanting you. Denying myself."

"Then stop denying yourself." Wes pushes back toward him, shameless, desperate. "Please, Stellan. I've wanted you just as long."

Jace's thumb finds my clit at the same moment Stellan positions himself at Wes's entrance. I'm trembling, caught between watching and feeling, overwhelmed by both.

"If we do this," Stellan says quietly, "you'll feel what I feel. Feeder to Feeder. No barriers."

"I know." Wes's voice is certain despite the desperation. "I want that. I want *you*."

Stellan pushes inside.

The sound Wes makes is *wrecked*—halfway between a sob and a moan, his whole body arching off the couch. Stellan is longer than Gray, I can tell from the way Wes's breath punches out, the way his hands scrabble for purchase.

I come without warning.

Jace's fingers, Stellan sinking into Wes, the Feeder magic starting to pulse through the bond—it all crashes together and I'm clenching around Jace's hand, gasping, my whole body shaking.

"There you go," Jace breathes, fucking me through it with his fingers. "That's one. Let's see how many more we can get while you watch."

"Oh god—" Wes gasps from the couch. "Oh fuck, you're—I can feel—"

"Yes." Stellan bottoms out, hips flush against Wes's ass, and holds there. His eyes have gone dark, his jaw clenched. "You feel that? Your hunger and mine, recognizing each other."

The magic in the room *shifts*.

I feel it through the bond—this warm pulse of energy that starts in my chest and radiates outward. Wes is feeding, but not the way he does with me or Gray. He's feeding *with* Stellan, their power tangling together, creating something that feels like a live wire in my bloodstream.

"Oh fuck," Jace breathes against my neck, his fingers stilling inside me. "What *is* that?"

"Feeder sync," Theo says from somewhere nearby, his voice strained. "When two of them connect during sex, it creates a feedback loop. Pleasure amplifying pleasure."

Stellan starts to fuck him.

It's not gentle or careful. But deep, driving thrusts that have Wes crying out with every one, his cock bouncing untouched, precome dripping onto the couch beneath him. Stellan's hands grip his hips with bruising force, centuries of control finally cracking.

Jace resumes his rhythm inside me, matching Stellan's pace, and I'm caught between watching and feeling—every thrust into Wes echoed by Jace's fingers curling inside me.

"Do you know how long I've wanted this?" Stellan's voice has gone ragged, nothing like his usual elegant composure. "How many times I watched you with Gray and imagined it was me? Imagined being inside you, making you make these sounds—"

"Stellan—" Wes is barely coherent. "Please, I need—I'm so close—"

"Not yet." Stellan slows his thrusts, pulling almost all the way out before sinking back in. Wes *whines*. "I want to feel you break first. I want to feel it through the bond."

The feedback loop spikes so hard my knees buckle. Jace catches me, his free arm wrapping around my waist, holding me up while his other hand keeps working me. From the armchair, Rhett makes a low sound—watching all of it, watching me fall apart while watching them.

Stellan reaches around and wraps his hand around Wes's cock—finally, *finally*—and strokes him in time with his thrusts. Once. Twice. Three times.

Wes *screams*.

He comes so hard his whole body convulses, clamping down on Stellan's cock, shooting across the couch and the floor. The orgasm seems to last forever, his body jerking with aftershocks, Stellan fucking him through every wave.

"Yes," Stellan groans. "Yes, give it to me, let me feel it—"

He buries himself deep and follows Wes over, coming with a sound that doesn't match his elegant reputation at all—raw and broken and utterly *human*. Through the bond, I feel the echo of their shared climax, and I come again around Jace's fingers—harder this time, sobbing through it.

"That's two," Jace murmurs, sounding wrecked himself. "Fuck, you're beautiful when you come."

The aftershocks ripple through all of us. Theo's hand finds my shoulder, grounding. Even the room itself seems to pulse with residual energy.

Gray gathers Wes up when Stellan finally pulls out, arranging him on the couch with careful hands, murmuring praise into his hair. Stellan stays close, one hand resting on Wes's ankle—maintaining contact, maintaining the connection.

Jace slides his fingers out of me slowly, and I whimper at the loss.

"Go," he says, pressing a kiss to my shoulder. "I know you want to check on him."

"What about you?"

His grin is crooked, a little vulnerable underneath the bravado. "I'll be fine. Plenty of night left."

I start toward the couch, but I don't make it three steps before a warm hand catches my wrist.

Rhett.

He's finally moved from his armchair, and when he pulls me toward him, his skin is furnace-hot the way it gets when he's been holding back. His hazel eyes are dark, intent, cataloging every tremor still running through my body.

"My turn," he says. Not a question.

"Rhett—"

"I've been watching." He backs me toward the wall, slow and deliberate. "Watching Theo take you apart with his mouth. Watching you come on

Jace's fingers while you tried to focus on Wes. Watching your face when Stellan finally broke."

My back hits the wall. His hands bracket my hips, radiating heat that sinks into my bones.

"I know exactly what you need right now." His mouth brushes my ear. "You need something steady. Something that burns slow instead of fast."

He lifts me like I weigh nothing, and I wrap my legs around his waist on instinct. The head of his cock nudges my entrance—when did he get his pants off?—and I'm so wet from Jace, from watching, from *everything*, that he slides in with one smooth thrust.

I gasp. He's thick, stretching me perfectly, and the *heat* of him inside me is almost too much. His fire magic pulses through the bond, warming me from the inside out.

"There," he breathes against my throat. "That's what you needed."

He doesn't fuck me fast. He fucks me *deep*—long, rolling thrusts that hit something profound every time, his hips grinding against my clit at the apex of each stroke. His hands are branding hot on my thighs, and everywhere he touches leaves trails of warmth that linger.

"You're so beautiful like this," he murmurs. "Wrecked and still wanting more. Still taking everything we give you."

"Rhett—" I'm already close again, oversensitive and overwhelmed. "I can't—"

"You can." He picks up the pace, just slightly, his cock dragging against my walls in a way that makes my toes curl. "One more for me. I've been waiting all night."

His thumb finds my clit, pressing and circling in time with his thrusts, and the heat intensifies—his magic or just him, I can't tell anymore. The warmth spreads through my belly, my chest, pooling low and building.

"That's it." His voice is rough now, strained. "Come on my cock, firefly. Let me feel it."

The nickname breaks me.

I come with a sob, clenching around him so hard he groans, his hips stuttering. He follows me over with a low curse, spilling inside me in hot pulses that I swear I can feel warming me from the inside.

We stay there for a long moment, me pinned to the wall, him buried deep, both of us breathing hard.

"Okay?" he asks finally, pressing a kiss to my forehead.

"More than." I laugh weakly. "God, you weren't kidding about filing things away."

"I never kid about you." He eases out slowly, lowering me to my feet with careful hands. His come drips down my thighs, hot like the rest of him. "Go check on Wes. I know you want to."

I drift toward the couch, drawn by the sight of Wes looking so thoroughly undone. Gray has him cradled against his chest, but Wes's eyes find mine when I approach—dark and hazy and still hungry despite everything.

"Hi," he breathes.

"Hi yourself." I settle on the edge of the couch, brush damp curls off his forehead. "You look wrecked."

"Feel wrecked." His mouth curves. "In the best way."

Thane appears behind me. I feel him before I see him—that cool presence, the weight of centuries pressing against my spine. I turn to look at him and he's looking at Wes with an expression I can't quite read. Hunger. Recognition. *Want.*

"You fed well," Thane says. Not a question.

"Stellan—" Wes starts.

"I know. I felt it through the loop." Thane's voice drops lower, intimate. "Every pulse. Every wave. Every time you crested. I felt your cock twitch. Felt your hole clench around him. Felt you break apart."

Wes's breath catches. So does mine.

Something shifts in the air between them.

I've watched them circle each other for four years. Two Feeders, two kinds of hunger, and me in the middle pretending not to notice the tension. They've shared me before—Thane drinking from my throat while Wes fucked me, Wes feeding on our connection while Thane made me come. But they've never touched each other.

Gray's arms loosen around Wes, giving space. Stellan shifts back, giving room.

"What do you want?" Wes asks, and his voice has steadied now, something sharper underneath the haze.

Thane kneels beside the couch, silver eyes fixed on Wes like he's the only thing in the room. "To stop wondering."

My breath catches. God, his *voice.*

"Bree." Wes's eyes find mine. "Is this okay?"

"Are you kidding?" I manage. "I've imagined this probably a hundred times."

Thane's mouth twitches. "Only a hundred?"

"Shut up and kiss him."

So he does.

It's nothing like Thane's kisses with me—controlled, deliberate, designed to take me apart. This is two predators finally dropping their guards, and it's *savage*. Thane's hand fists in Wes's hair, yanking his head back, and Wes growls into his mouth—actually *growls*—and then they're devouring each other. Teeth and tongue and four years of denied want pouring out at once.

"Holy shit," Jace breathes from somewhere behind me.

Gray shifts, giving them more room, and his eyes are dark with something that isn't jealousy. *Pride*, I realize. He's proud of Wes for taking this. For claiming something he wanted.

When they finally break apart, both of them are breathing hard. Thane's composure is cracked—not shattered, but *cracked*—and Wes looks like he's been struck by lightning.

"Four years," Thane says roughly. "I should have done that four years ago."

Wes laughs, weak and wondering. "Yeah. You should have."

Thane's hand cups Wes's jaw with a tenderness that makes my chest ache. His thumb traces Wes's lower lip, swollen from the kiss.

"This isn't finished," Thane says quietly. "You know that."

"I know."

They don't kiss again. They don't need to. Something has shifted between them—a door that was locked for years now standing open. Whatever comes next, whenever it comes, they both know it's coming.

I'm so turned on I can barely breathe.

Seth crosses the room to collect me.

"Your turn," he says, and there's heat in his eyes but also patience. "If you want."

"I want."

He leads me to the wide chaise near the windows—big enough for three, which becomes relevant when Thane follows us over.

Not asking. Just present. Already done with Wes but not done for the night.

Seth doesn't tense. Four years ago, he would have—would have seen Thane as competition, as threat, as someone trying to take what was his. Now he just shifts to make room.

"Both of you?" I ask, and my voice comes out breathier than I intended.

"If you want," Thane says. His silver eyes are dark with hunger. "We've discussed it."

"You've—wait, you talked about this?"

"Occasionally." Seth's mouth quirks. "When you're not around."

The image hits me—the two of them, heads bent together, talking about *me*, about *this*, planning how they'd take me apart together. Heat floods through me.

"Yes," I manage. "Gods, yes."

Seth pulls me into his lap, my back to his chest, and Thane kneels between my spread thighs. For a moment, no one moves.

Then Thane leans in—but not toward me.

He kisses Seth.

It's not brief this time. It's deep and filthy, tongue and teeth, and Seth groans into it while I watch from inches away. Thane's hand comes up to grip Seth's jaw, angling him deeper, and Seth's cock twitches against my ass.

"Holy shit," I whisper.

Thane pulls back, lips wet, eyes blazing. "You like that."

It's not a question. He can probably smell how much I liked it.

"Do it again."

Thane's smile is sharp. "Bossy."

But he does it again—kisses Seth over my shoulder, deeper this time, dirtier. Seth's hands tighten on my hips, pulling me back against him, and I can feel how hard he is through his pants, his cock straining against the fabric and pressing into the curve of my ass.

Thane's hand slides between my thighs while he's still kissing Seth. His fingers find me—soaked, ruined—and he makes a low sound of approval into Seth's mouth.

"She's dripping," Thane says when he finally pulls back, his lips wet and swollen. "Just from watching us kiss."

"Told you she would be." Seth's voice is rough. His hips roll up against me, grinding his cock against my ass. "She's been thinking about this for months."

"Years," I correct breathlessly. "I've been thinking about this for years."

"Then let's stop making you wait."

Seth's hands slide over my hips, pulling me more firmly against him while Thane watches with those silver eyes that see everything. Thane reaches out and traces one finger down the center of my body—between my breasts, over my stomach, stopping just above where I'm aching for him.

"Beautiful," he murmurs. "Every time, I forget how beautiful you are like this."

"Thane—"

"Patience." He looks at Seth over my shoulder. "Get inside her. I want to watch."

Seth doesn't need to be told twice. He lifts me, positions me, and then he's pulling me down onto his cock—thick and hot and stretching me open in one long slide.

I moan, head falling back against his shoulder. Seth is big—they all are, but Seth fills me in a way that always makes me feel *claimed*. Like he's leaving his mark inside me just by being there.

"That's it," Seth breathes against my neck. "Fuck, Bree. You feel so good. Always so tight, no matter how many times—"

"Move," I beg. "Please, I need—"

"Not yet." Thane's hand on my hip stills me. "I want a taste first."

And then he drops to his knees in front of us.

Oh *fuck*.

His mouth finds me where Seth and I are joined—tongue dragging through my folds, circling my clit, tracing the stretched rim of where Seth's cock is buried inside me. I nearly scream, my whole body jerking, and Seth swears viciously behind me.

"Jesus Christ, Thane—"

"I can feel you both," Thane murmurs against me, the vibration of his voice making me clench. "Taste you both. Her arousal and your precome, mixing together—" His tongue flicks my clit and I sob. "—it's intoxicating."

He seals his mouth over my clit and *sucks*, and I shatter.

The orgasm rips through me without warning, my pussy clamping down on Seth's cock, my whole body convulsing. Seth groans and holds me through it, his cock twitching inside me, clearly fighting not to come.

Thane doesn't stop.

He keeps licking, keeps sucking, working me through the aftershocks and then pushing me toward another peak. His tongue slides down to where Seth is stretching me, tracing the place where we're connected, and Seth's hips buck involuntarily—fucking up into me, pushing me into Thane's mouth.

"Thane—" Seth's voice is wrecked. "If you keep doing that I'm gonna come down your throat."

Thane pulls back just enough to look up at us, his mouth slick, lips swollen, his eyes blazing silver. "Would that be a problem?"

"*Fuck.*"

"Later, perhaps." Thane's smile is wicked. "Right now, I have other plans."

He rises fluidly, and I see him for the first time—really see him. He's hard, his cock straining against his pants, longer than Seth's but not as thick. Different. They're all different, and I love knowing exactly how each of them feels inside me.

"I want to be inside you too," Thane says. "Both of us at once. Can you take that?"

My pussy clenches around Seth at just the thought. "Yes. Gods, yes. Please."

Thane strips efficiently—no show, just necessity—and then he's there, pressing against me from the front while Seth holds me from behind. Two cocks, two men, both of them hard and leaking and desperate to be inside me.

Thane produces lube, slicks himself up, and positions himself at my entrance alongside Seth.

"Breathe," he instructs. "Relax. Let us in."

The pressure is intense—too much, impossible. I breathe out, consciously relaxing my muscles, and Thane pushes forward.

The stretch is *obscene*.

I cry out as he sinks in, inch by impossible inch, my body struggling to accommodate both of them. Seth is groaning behind me, his grip bruising on my hips, and I can tell from the way he's shaking that he can feel Thane's cock sliding against his own.

"So full," I gasp. "I'm so full, I can't—"

"You can." Thane's voice is strained but certain. "You're taking us so well. Just a little more."

He bottoms out, and for a moment, all three of us just breathe.

The room has gone quiet. I'm dimly aware of the others watching—Gray with Wes still tucked against him on the couch, Stellan's hand frozen on Wes's ankle, Rhett leaning forward in his chair, Jace for once in his life not saying a word. Theo's eyes are dark and fixed on us like he's memorizing every detail.

"Holy fuck," Jace finally breathes. "That's the hottest thing I've ever seen."

"Shut *up*, Jace," I manage, but there's no heat in it.

"Never." But his voice is rougher than usual, awed instead of teasing.

I've never felt anything like this. Two cocks inside me, stretching me to my limit, pressed so tightly together they can feel every twitch and pulse of each other. When Seth shifts, Thane groans. When Thane clenches, Seth swears. We're connected—all three of us—in the most intimate way possible.

"Move," I beg. "Please, I need you to move."

They start slowly, carefully—Seth pulling back as Thane pushes in, Thane withdrawing as Seth thrusts up. The friction is unreal, both of them dragging against my inner walls, never leaving me empty. I'm making sounds I don't recognize, high desperate keening noises, my nails raking down Thane's back.

"Faster," I plead. "Harder. I can take it."

"You sure?" Seth's voice is barely controlled.

"*Fuck me.*"

Something snaps.

They stop being careful. Thane slams into me as Seth drives up, and I *scream*—not in pain, in overwhelming pleasure. They find a brutal rhythm, alternating thrusts that keep me constantly full, constantly stimulated, every nerve ending in my body on fire.

"That's it," Thane growls against my ear. "Take us. Take everything we give you. You were made for this—made to be filled by us, fucked by us, *owned* by us—"

"Yes—" I can barely speak, can barely think. "Yes, yes, please—"

Seth's hand finds my clit, rubbing in tight circles as they fuck me, and something inside me snaps.

Not breaks—*releases*.

The orgasm doesn't crash over me. It pulls me under. My vision whites out, my hearing goes distant, and my body stops being mine. I'm shaking—or maybe convulsing—clamping down on both of them so hard they groan in unison, but I can't respond because I'm not *here* anymore. I'm just sensation. Just nerve endings firing and muscles clenching and wave after wave after wave that won't stop coming.

Somewhere far away, I hear myself making sounds. Not words. Not moans. Something raw and broken and animal.

Tears are streaming down my face. I can feel them, hot and wet, but I can't stop them. Can't stop any of it. My body is moving on autopilot—clenching, rolling, taking—while the rest of me floats somewhere outside of it, shattered into pieces I'm not sure I can put back together.

"Jesus Christ," someone says. Jace, maybe. Or Rhett. I can't tell.

"She's gone," Seth breathes against my neck, awed. "Thane, she's completely—"

"I know." Thane's voice is wrecked. "I can feel it. *Fuck*, I can feel everything."

"Fuck, I can't—" Seth's rhythm stutters.

Seth buries himself deep and comes with a shout, his cock pulsing, flooding me with heat. The sensation of his release triggers Thane—I feel him swell impossibly bigger before he slams in one final time and spills.

Two cocks throbbing inside me. Two loads of come filling me at once. The bond blazes so bright I can't see, can't think, can't do anything but shake through an orgasm that seems to last forever.

From the couch, Wes makes a broken sound and the Feeder magic spikes one final time, pleasure echoing through all of us, connecting us, binding us together.

When it finally ebbs, I'm sobbing.

Not from sadness. From *overwhelm*. From being so thoroughly claimed, so completely loved, that my body doesn't know what to do with it.

"Shh," Thane murmurs, pressing kisses to my temple, my cheek, the corner of my mouth. "We have you. We've got you."

"That was..." Seth sounds as wrecked as I feel. "That was..."

"Yeah," Thane agrees. "It was."

The room settles into aftermath.

Not all at once—there's no clean ending, no moment where everyone stops. Just a gradual slowing, bodies untangling and retangling in different configurations.

Wes is still on the couch, sandwiched between Gray and Stellan, looking thoroughly wrecked and completely content. Stellan's hand has found his ankle again. Gray's fingers are back in his hair. Something has shifted between the three of them—something that was always there but finally got spoken aloud.

Jace is sprawled in the armchair now, looking thoroughly debauched even though he never got off—his pants are still undone from earlier, his hair a mess, his mouth swollen from kisses I didn't see him steal. When Stellan catches his eye, something passes between them—a question, maybe, or an answer. Jace's mouth curves into something softer than his usual grin.

"Later," Stellan says quietly.

"Yeah," Jace agrees. "Later."

Rhett is back in his spot near the fireplace, sprawled out and looking thoroughly satisfied. He catches me looking and his smile goes warm and knowing.

"Best view in the house," he says. "Told you."

"You watched most of it."

"I watched all of it. Even when I had you against the wall, I was still paying attention to the rest of the room." His smile widens. "Watched Seth and Thane fuck you at the same time until you cried. I know exactly what makes each of you fall apart."

"And you file it all away."

"And I use it." His eyes darken with promise. "Like I did with you earlier. You think I didn't notice how you react when someone calls you by a nickname? When someone tells you exactly what they need from you?"

My face heats. "Rhett—"

"I'm not complaining, firefly." The nickname makes my breath catch, proving his point. "I'm just saying—I pay attention. And I remember everything."

"That's—"

"Hot," Jace supplies from the armchair. "The word you're looking for is hot."

"I was going to say intense."

"Same thing."

Thane eases out of me carefully, and Seth follows, and the sudden emptiness makes me whimper. But then they're both there—Thane pressing a kiss to my forehead, Seth pulling me against his chest—and the emptiness fills with something else.

They share a look over my head. Something has shifted between them too—the last wall crumbling, the last distance closed. They've been inside me together. They've kissed. They've felt each other.

There's no going back from that. No pretending they're just two men who happen to love the same woman.

Thane brings water. Actual glasses of water, distributed to whoever reaches for them, because even ancient vampires understand the importance of hydration. He presses one into my hands without being asked.

"Drink."

"Thanks, mom."

"Don't test me."

I drink.

Seth keeps me tucked against him on the chaise, one hand tracing lazy patterns on my hip. He likes staying close after—says it helps him believe it really happened. I used to think that was sad. Now I just settle into it, let him have what he needs.

"Theo really did a number on you," Seth observes, pressing a kiss to my hair.

"He does that."

"I know. I'm not complaining." His arms tighten around me. "I like it. Getting you after you've already fallen apart once. You're so much more... open."

"Is that your way of saying I have control issues?"

"That's my way of saying I love you."

Eventually, we migrate to the bedroom.

The massive bed that cost more than my old apartment's yearly rent—custom-made to fit everyone, because apparently that's a thing you can just order—is a mess of bodies and blankets within minutes.

I end up in the middle. Not because I put myself there; because they arrange around me, the same way they always do, like I'm the point every-thing orients toward.

But it doesn't feel like pressure anymore. Doesn't feel like responsibility.

It just feels like home.

"Mira's going to want pancakes," Jace mumbles, face smushed into someone's shoulder. "I'm calling it now."

"It's three in the morning," Wes points out.

"She doesn't care. She's three. Time is meaningless."

"You're making them, then."

"Obviously I'm making them. I always make them." Jace yawns. "Holy-shit-we're-alive pancakes. It's tradition at this point."

Something warm blooms in my chest. He's been making those pancakes since the beginning—since that first impossible night when everything changed and he stood at a stove at dawn, cracking eggs like the world hadn't just turned inside out.

"I'll help," Rhett offers from the outer edge of the pile.

"You'll eat them before they hit the plate."

"That's helping. Quality control."

"That's the most romantic thing you've ever said to me."

"Shut up and go to sleep."

Thane makes a sound that might be a sigh or might be an exhausted laugh. "Four years," he says, to no one in particular. "I've survived four years of this."

"Survived?" Stellan's voice is dry. "You love it."

"I tolerate it."

"You made water appear out of nowhere to make sure everyone stayed hydrated."

"Basic caretaking. Don't read into it."

Seth snorts against my hair. "He's such a soft touch."

"I will end you."

"You literally just tucked a blanket around Wes."

"He was cold."

"You checked if he was cold first. You *asked*."

"I'm surrounded by idiots."

I'm laughing. I don't even know when it started, but I'm laughing, this exhausted, full-body laughter that makes my stomach hurt and my eyes sting. Theo squeezes my hand. Gray presses a kiss to my shoulder. Seth holds me tighter.

"This is ridiculous," I manage. "All of you. This whole situation. It's completely ridiculous."

"Absolutely," Jace agrees. "But it's ours."

The monitor on the nightstand glows green. Both lights steady. Both kids asleep, blissfully unaware that their parents are a chaotic tangle of limbs in a bed that shouldn't technically exist.

Eight men. Two kids. One life that shouldn't work but does.

If someone had told me this was possible—that I could have this, feel this safe and this wanted—I would have laughed in their face.

Then probably cried.

Then definitely run.

Thank god no one told me.

Thank god I found out for myself.

THE END

THANK YOU

I promised myself I wouldn't cry writing this.

I'm already crying.

Look, I knew this was coming. I've known for five books that this was where we'd end up—Bree standing in front of that attic door, finally whole enough to close it. Finally choosing herself. Finally home.

I still wasn't ready.

Here's something most people don't know: I rewrote this series three times.

Three times. Different plots. Different villains. Different paths to get Bree where she needed to go. I restructured everything, threw out entire books, started over from scratch more than once. Threw away Raith who WILL show up in a future something. Because my god that man is sexy in my head and I need to share him with you.

But book one never changed.

Crown of the Mist was always the beginning. Always Bree in that house, discovering magic was real, finding out the boys she'd loved forever had loved her back. That story knew what it was from the first draft. Everything else had to catch up.

The Ether Chronicles started as a question: *What if the broken girl got to keep everything?* Not just survive. Not just heal. But actually, genuinely *have* it all—the love, the family, the happily ever after that felt impossible.

Bree was never supposed to be this big. She was supposed to be a side character in something else entirely. A footnote. A girl with too much trauma and not enough hope.

But she wouldn't shut up.

She kept talking in my head. Kept showing me who she really was underneath all that armor. Kept insisting she deserved more than I was giving her.

So I gave her everything.

Eight men who loved her without conditions. A crown she never asked for. A sanctuary that grew around her like the world itself was trying to keep her safe. Crystalline daisies that chimed in the wind because her magic remembered beauty even when she'd forgotten how to see it.

And you.

I gave her you.

You showed up. Book after book, you came back. You screamed at Phil (valid). You fell for Thane even when you knew better (also valid). You sent me messages at 2am asking if Seth was okay, if Bree was okay, if *you* were going to be okay after what I'd just put you through.

(The answer was always: eventually. I'm not a monster. Mostly.)

Because that's what this series is really about, isn't it? Not the battles. Not the villains. Not even the victories.

It's about what comes after.

It's about standing in the wreckage and choosing to rebuild. About showing up to eighteen funerals because the dead deserve witnesses. About forgiving someone who hurt you—not because they earned it, but because carrying the anger was heavier than letting it go.

It's about closing the door on who you were so you can finally become who you're meant to be.

Bree closes that attic door at the end. The crown is still there. The power is still there. But she doesn't need to claim it right now. She's done putting herself last.

That scene made me cry harder than anything else I wrote.

Because *that's* the real victory. Not defeating the monster. Choosing yourself.

Three rewrites. Six books. One story that refused to let me tell it wrong.

Thank you for letting me tell it at all.

Thank you for loving Bree when she couldn't love herself. For trusting me with her heart and yours. For staying through the grief and the healing and the frankly ridiculous amount of spicy content once we got to it (you're welcome, by the way).

Thank you for making this series everything I dreamed it could be and more.

The Ether Chronicles are done. Bree is happy. The sanctuary is thriving. Somewhere in that absurdly large bed, eight men are fighting over who has to make holy-shit-we're-alive pancakes.

But I'm not done. Not even close. I've got more stories, more chaos, more fictional men who will absolutely ruin your dating standards.

For now, though—for Bree, for her boys, for the daisies that still chime in the garden—

Thank you.

From the bottom of my chaotic, sleep-deprived, hopelessly romantic heart.

-Zora

About the Author

Zora Stone writes romantasy with teeth: fierce heroines, protective men who'd burn the world for them, and enough emotional wreckage to keep things interesting. When she's not plotting betrayals or steamy chaos, she's drinking iced coffee, dodging laundry, or daydreaming about enchanted forests.

You can find her online at:

Website: ZoraStone.com

TikTok | Instagram: @ZoraStoneAuthor

And on Amazon and Goodreads.

Want behind-the-scenes chaos and sneak peeks? ZoraStone.com/Influencers

ALSO BY ZORA STONE

The Ether Chronicles

Crown of the Mist
Into the Ether
Ashen Oath
Veil of Echoes
Shattering the Void
To the Final End

Arcanum Academy

Shadows of Change
Shadows Rising
Shadows Found

Shadows Revealed